Cover Copy

Beware of the Pirate Prince is the sweet/tame version of Her Pirate Prince.

My dearest Anteros,

As the daughter of an English earl, I grew up sheltered and protected, then I became your bride, the wife of a prince born with untold secrets and untold pirate tendencies.

Luckily, I adore both the prince you are, and the devious pirate that simmers under your skin.

Unluckily, you've enraged your enemies, and now your greatest enemy, the Dey of Algiers, is forcing you into a battle unlike any you've ever fought. He has now captured me and made me the bait in his vile game to lure you to Algiers. Please, you must find me, rescue me, and eliminate the threat he's become to our family and our people. You must do so without getting either of us killed, because more than anything, I adore being your wife, and wish to remain so.

Be safe and take all care.

Forever yours, Olivia.

Books by Joanne Wadsworth

The Matheson Brothers Series

Highlander's Desire, Book 1
Highlander's Passion, Book 2
Highlander's Seduction, Book 3
Highlander's Kiss, Book 4
Highlander's Heart, Book 5
Highlander's Sword, Book 6
Highlander's Bride, Book 7
Highlander's Caress, Book 8
Highlander's Touch, Book 9
Highlander's Shifter, Book 10
Highlander's Claim, Book 11
Highlander's Courage, Book 12
Highlander's Mermaid, Book 13

Highlander Heat Series

Highlander's Castle, Book 1
Highlander's Magic, Book 2
Highlander's Charm, Book 3
Highlander's Guardian, Book 4
Highlander's Faerie, Book 5
Highlander's Champion, Book 6
Highlander's Captive, Novella 0.5

Princesses of Myth Series

Protector, Book 1
Warrior, Book 2
Hunter, Novella 2.5
Enchanter, Book 3
Healer, Book 4
Chaser, Book 5

Books by Joanne Wadsworth

Regency Brides Series
The Duke's Bride, Book 1
The Earl's Bride, Book 2
The Wartime Bride, Book 3
The Earl's Secret Bride, Book 4
The Prince's Bride, Book 5
Her Pirate Prince, Book 6
Chased by the Corsair, Book 7

Sweet Regency Tales
(Sweet/tame version of Regency Brides)
The Duke Who Stole My Heart, Book 1
The Earl I Adore, Book 2
To Love During War, Book 3
My Secret and the Earl, Book 4
The Prince Who Captured Me, Book 5
Beware of the Pirate Prince, Book 6
My Infamous Corsair, Book 7

Billionaire Bodyguards Series
Billionaire Bodyguard Attraction, Book 1
Billionaire Bodyguard Boss, Book 2
Billionaire Bodyguard Fling, Book 3

Beware of the Pirate Prince

(Pirates of the High Seas)
Sweet Regency Tales, Book 6

JOANNE WADSWORTH

Beware of the Pirate Prince
ISBN-13: 978-0-9951194-0-6
Copyright © 2020, Joanne Wadsworth
Cover Art by Joanne Wadsworth
First publication: June 2020

Joanne Wadsworth
http://www.joannewadsworth.com

AUTHOR'S NOTE:
This book is a work of fiction. The names, characters, places, and incidents are products of the writer's imagination or have been used fictitiously and are not to be construed as real. Any resemblance to persons, living or dead, actual events, locale or organizations is entirely coincidental. The author does not have any control over and does not assume any responsibility for third-party websites or their content.

Published in the United States of America

A Word From the Author

Each book within this series is standalone, although for your reading pleasure you may wish to read The Prince Who Captured Me (Sweet Regency Tales, Book 5) before this one, as this story is a continuing adventure for Prince Anteros and Olivia.

The Seer: Shira Ria

Under a midnight moon, her robes donned and hair of silver and white covered, Shira walked carefully along the craggy, treacherous edge of the cliffs of Algiers, the waves crashing into the shore far below, and the salty spray drifting through the humid night air. As the seer of Algiers, she *saw* far more than anyone else, and tonight, at the uppermost peak of the headland, a wispy white presence floated back and forth, visible only to her. The ghostly presence beckoned her, awaited her arrival. Mario of Paradiso. She sensed the urgency that had brought Mario to this rugged place this eve.

She touched the tinkling charms dangling from her wrist-full of silver bangles, the wind whipping through with unwavering strength. That wind threatened to tumble her down the cliffs and into the jagged rocks and unforgiving waters far below. This was such a dangerously magnificent place, where the silvery blackness of the water met the endless, starlight horizon of the Mediterranean Sea.

Taking a deep breath, she focused on Mario's spirit form and continued onward and upward. When she finally reached the upper crest, she stepped across a patch of rocky ground as his wispy being floated closer.

After another careful step, she cupped her palms around his cheeks, her dear friend having been gone these past thirteen years. Slowly, his form got stronger, the wispy whiteness becoming more solid. "*As-salamu alaykum.* It is good to see you, Mario."

"*Wa alaykum al-salam.* As it is to see you, Shira." Even with the whiteness, shadows lined his face.

"Why have you beckoned me here to these cliffs this eve? I see the worry etched upon your face."

"I've had a disturbing premonition of my grandson, Anteros, and his beloved new bride, Olivia."

"What have you seen?" Trepidation tightened her chest. She'd awoken last eve with sweat beading her brow from a vision that had jerked her abruptly from her sleep. The vision had been of Anteros and Olivia wading through a thick pool of congealed blood. Olivia had floundered and gotten sucked below the surface. Anteros had searched frantically for her, shoving the clotted blood away before he finally found her. He'd plucked her from the jellied mess, scooped her into his arms and slogged through the endless waves of bloodred toward Shira. He'd shouted her name, and she'd tried to reach out a hand to aid him, but Anteros had fallen back into the endless abyss of blood, Olivia going under with him.

"Olivia will soon be stolen away from Anteros." Mario leaned forward, raised one wispy eyebrow. "You've seen the pool of blood they get lost within?"

"I have, and it was a disturbing vision."

"It shall become their reality if you and I don't take action."

"Anteros would never allow any harm to come to Olivia. She is his very heart."

"A heart that his greatest enemy wishes to strike at." Mario's gaze narrowed. "The enemy I speak of is the Dey of Algiers. We both know how viciously Dey Hazim wishes to control all of the Mediterranean. He will obliterate anyone who stands in his path, of which Anteros stands front and center."

"I too have seen the same vicious need during readings I've done for the dey." She released a stuttered breath. "Mario, lately Hazim's corsairs have arrived back into port with more slaves than ever before in their holds. Not only do they raid merchant ships, but they also steal into villages all across these seas and take all the flesh they can. They care naught for who they seize, the rich or the poor, the educated or the uneducated. No one is exempt."

Bile rose in her throat. She'd always detested Hazim's foul means of taking and selling slaves. Goodness, but just last week along the bay, she'd stood on the verge of a large crowd that had clamored around the returning corsairs as the pirates had herded the unfortunate souls they'd captured off their ships.

Chained together in their torn and bloodied clothes, those poor souls had stumbled barefoot into the city. The corsairs had prodded the slaves with their scimitars, shouting with hoots and hollers and leery grins as they'd led them along the cobbled streets toward the slave pens belonging to Hazim.

In the past, she'd always done all she could for those captured, many-a-time having bartered readings with Hazim just for access into the pens. Once there, she'd always made her way to the children first, the most vulnerable, many of them stolen away from their parents. When tending to the children, she ensured they had blankets and food, and whatever else she could offer. "Hazim spreads his reign of terror across all these lands. I'm not sure what else I can do."

"I know you wish you could halt him, Shira."

"I do, more than I could ever express with words, but I don't have the means to do so. Only Anteros does. He has a large fleet of ships at his command, but I fear after the vision I've had, he too will be taken from us."

"We need to alter your vision, seek another outcome." Mario surrounded her with his wispy warmth. "Anteros sinks as many of Hazim's ships as he can. He often frees the slaves before they even reach Algiers, but it isn't enough. Not nearly enough. Hazim simply builds more ships and sends his corsairs back out to do his bidding." Mario motioned out toward the dark waves which swelled for as far as the eye could see, the ripples of white surf highlighted by the gentle glow of the moon. "Hazim is about to come after Anteros and all he holds dear. It's time for you to set a grand plan in motion, one that will free all those who need freeing."

"How do you propose I do that?"

"His house is divided, Shira. Hazim's two sons stand either side of that divide, and as we are both aware—"

"—a divided house cannot stand," Shira finished with a firm nod.

"Correct." Mario placed his palms together in a prayerful stance. "There is an evilness which pervades Hazim's soul, the same as it does with his second-born son, Barossa."

"I've seen that evilness, but it doesn't pervade Nazari's soul, Hazim's firstborn son." She touched her heart and continued, "Nazari's mother had a soft and loving heart. He holds the same."

"Nazari is different to his father and half-brother. I've seen the same as you." Mario turned toward the palace sitting high on the terraced hilltop overlooking the citadel, the elegant, sprawling white structure two stories high with a succession of curved arches supported by pillars and topped with a crowned roof and raised domes, the dey's flag flapping in the nighttime breeze from the uppermost point of his fortress.

"What else do you see?" she asked Mario. "Share with me all you can."

"If Anteros and Olivia are to survive what's coming for them, then you must read Anteros's future, for only once you have will you truly know what to do. They can't be allowed to perish. Devise a plan. I have every faith in you."

"I won't fail you." Or any of her loved ones.

"Summon Anteros and read his future. Summon Adrestia too. Anteros will need his sister during the difficult days to come." Fine tendrils separated from his form and swirled all about her. His love encompassed her for a brief moment before his essence floated out over the cliffs where nothing but the sea raged far below. "*Ma al-salamah*." He blew her a kiss. "Take care of our loved ones."

"*Ila al-liqaa*, Mario. Of course, I shall." She blew him a kiss in return, and the wind rose and sent the last of his form shimmering away on the breeze.

He was gone, although she wasn't alone. She would never be alone.

A Summons For Anteros

Dearest Anteros,
Your grandfather came to me.
He connected in his spirit form.
You must come to me as he instructed.
We have much to speak about.
In secret, out on the water.
Bring Adrestia.
Leave Olivia at home.

Follow my instructions precisely.
Do not waver from my request.
We must change the course of yours and Olivia's
future.
We must intervene against death.

Habeebi, *much love,*
Shira.

Every Drop In the Ocean Has a Story to Tell

Two days after receipt of the summons, one mile along the coastline from the Kasbah of Algiers, late 1811.

Anteros turned the skiff's oar a touch to ensure the strong current within the bay didn't carry him any farther out to sea. He'd rowed to this exact spot after receiving a letter of summons from Shira to collect her in secret. He'd also brought his sister as Shira had requested, leaving Olivia at home on the island of Paradiso.

That had been the hardest thing he'd ever done.

A man should never be separated from his new bride, and certainly not when said bride had a tendency of getting into trouble. Now, more than ever, he needed to keep Olivia in his sight, particularly considering the last line of Shira's summons stating they needed to intervene against death.

From his position on the center seat of the skiff—the sun ablaze and the desert sands inland burning a vivid orange hue—he gave the wise woman he considered family his full attention. "Shira, you may speak freely."

"*Lahda men fadlek.*" Shira held up a staying hand, her gaze going to his loyal right-hand man and crew keeping an alert eye on the coastline from *The Cobra's* deck. "All appears clear," she stated. "I must apologize."

"No apology is needed." He scanned the citadel's northern stone wall facing the sea where a succession of cannons ran the entire curved length, the city itself rising into the hills, the pastel-colored dwellings all densely packed together behind the fortified walls. Higher along the terraces, narrow alleyways twisted and turned, the stronghold of Algiers governed by the almighty Dey of Algiers—Dey Hazim, his greatest enemy. "Hazim's cannons can't reach us here. Tell me what you've seen to have sent the summons."

"Far too much, yet also not nearly enough." Shira wrapped an arm around Adrestia's shoulders. The two of them had always been close, like grandmother and granddaughter, their bond tight.

Adrestia wrapped an arm around Shira's shoulders in return. "I miss Grandfather terribly. I wish he'd visit me in his spirit form."

"Oh, my sweet girl, even though you can't see your grandfather, he still watches over you and Anteros. Mario will always be near, for those we've loved and lost are never truly far away. We are separated by a thin veil alone."

"I'll be forever grateful he raised us." Adrestia's voice

hitched. "It doesn't matter how many years he's been gone. Sometimes it feels like yesterday that he passed away."

"It feels the same way for me too." He reached across and squeezed his sister's arm. His grandfather had oozed vitality, right up until the last few months of his life before he'd breathed his last. "We were born during a difficult time for our parents. Our father feared for his monarchy and the continued reign of the Royal House of Bourbon."

"Grandfather offered us a sanctuary." The wind rose and rippled the soft linen of his sister's scarlet tunic belted over a pair of tan breeches. With her booted feet resting in the hull, a little water sloshing about, she eyed Shira. "When did you first meet our father?"

"Well before either of you two were born." Shira lifted the hem of her white robes from the water where one edge draped into it. "He was seventeen, already the King of Naples and Sicily. Ferdinand had heard of my ability. When he visited for readings, he preferred not alerting Dey Hazim to his arrival."

"A wise decision." With another turn of the oar, he kept them in position over the rising swell of the waves. "Let's not alert him today either."

"Agreed." Shira shuffled forward on the bench, the waves slapping against the sides of the skiff. "Anteros, during your grandfather's visit, he asked me to read your future."

"Then that's what you should do." Setting his oars aside, he held out his palm. "We also don't know how much time we have left. Do it now."

"I'll need both palms, and a conduit. Water will do." Shira leaned over the side of the skiff and scooped a

handful of seawater.

He cupped both palms together and she tipped the water in. It sloshed about, then slowly settled with a few salty bubbles popping on the top.

"Perfect." She gave a firm nod. "Now, release the water very slowly. Leave only the sandy grains behind for me to read."

"Of course." He allowed a trickle through.

"Let me see your palms." Shira took ahold of his hands and studied the remaining grains. "Hmm, I see deceit and distrust. I see blood falling. I see Nazari."

"Wait. Nazari? Are you sure?" He frowned. "That cannot be right. What has Nazari got to do with all of this?"

"I definitely see Nazari. The two of you are linked, have always been linked." She searched the grains again, then locked gazes with him. "I realize he is Hazim's son, but there was a time when you and Nazari trusted each other. That trust must come back into play, a friendship lost but once more restored. That is what I see in your future."

"He is a betrayer, Shira. I will never trust Nazari again."

"You two must set your differences aside if you wish to bring Hazim to heel. Remember, even though they are father and son, their relationship was altered intrinsically upon the death of Nazari's mother. Nazari still mourns her, will always mourn her. And he despises the role his father had in her demise."

"Will that 'despise' be enough to turn Nazari to my side?"

"Nazari cannot rid himself of his father without your aid, Anteros. If you and Nazari remove Hazim from this world, then you remove the threat Hazim poses to you and Olivia. Do you wish to save her life and yours?"

"Of course." Without a doubt, he did.

"Anteros!" Giovani shouted his name across the water, then motioned to a watchman riding along the ridge with sand flying from his horse's hooves. "The rider has spotted us and returns to the city to raise the alert."

"I see him!" he shouted back before facing Shira. "We're running out of time."

"We are, but I've seen all I need to see. I must speak to Nazari. I must devise a plan to save you all. I'll send him to you the moment I have a plan prepared. Await his arrival on Paradiso." Shira handed him the oars. *"Yajebu an athhaba al aan.* Return me to the shore."

Chapter 1

A week later, Paradiso Island in the Mediterranean Sea.

Anteros still awaited Nazari's arrival. He wouldn't dwell on it today though. He would enjoy this outing with Olivia. Galloping around the curve of the beach, he urged his jet-black Arabian stallion on, his beast's powerful hooves spitting out grainy white sands behind them, the crystal-clear waves of the sea crashing into the shore. Overhead, the skies blazed a warm blue while in front of him, his precious new bride raised her hands high, her golden hair whipping back as she giggled.

"This is a breathtaking ride." She sighed with delight as she rested her head back against his shoulder. "I'd forgotten what it's like to be outside since you've been keeping me confined within the castello since you returned."

"I didn't wish to have you out of my sight." He'd

doubled his guardsmen patrolling the castello and the shoreline and attended to other areas of defense. No one would breach his safe haven. Burrowing his nose in Olivia's golden locks, he breathed in her enticing orange blossom scent. This afternoon's excursion now gave him the chance to spend some precious time alone with her, time which he'd been desperately missing while tending to their security. Bringing her to this secluded part of the island would ensure their complete privacy. Straightening in his saddle, he lifted his chin and guided his horse around the bend of the beach toward the headland where the waves crashed into the boulders and sent spray misting into the air.

"When do you think Nazari will arrive?" She half turned toward him.

"Shira did not state the day or time."

"Adrestia said some women find him charming, although she gagged as she spoke those words. I gather they've had a difficult relationship?"

"That is saying it mildly. Nazari is Hazim's son, a devil in disguise."

"Yet Shira considers Nazari one of her beloved children."

"It's all rather perplexing, isn't it?"

"Yes, which makes me wonder how you and Nazari became friends?"

"That happened through Shira. She means the world to both of us."

"How long has Shira known him?"

"His entire life. Shira was there for Nazari's birth, aided him through the days after his mother's death when he was but a boy of five, and has been there for him ever since."

"Five? That's terrible. No child should ever lose their mother at such a young age."

"You feel compassion for him?"

"I don't even know him." She cupped his cheek. "Anteros, no child should be defined by who their parents are, which is why I'm so curious about him."

"You'll have to save your curiosity for another time. We're almost there."

"Almost where?"

"Where Paradiso first began. Look ahead." He gestured to where the beach ended, the sun glinting off the waves with bright brilliance.

"All I see is the sea."

"That's because we're about to enter it to reach the place I'm taking you to."

"Pardon? Wait!" She shrieked as he steered his horse directly into the pounding surf. "Anteros, you can't ride into the sea."

"I certainly can." He urged his mount deeper and deeper into the waves and laughed as Olivia tried to rise up out of the saddle. "Where are you going, *mio angelo*?" He caught her around the waist, kept her pinned to his lap.

"I'm getting wet, Anteros, and, and—" Shock coursed across her sweet face as she stared at the waves rolling past them, his horse's hooves no longer touching the seabed. "Fedele can swim?"

"All horses can."

"I never knew." Wide-eyed, she giggled with excitement. "Papa was remiss in teaching me this when I first learned to ride."

"Fedele can actually swim far faster than any of the other horses in my stables. He's a clever beast." Waves sloshed over his lap then retreated as he pushed Fedele even faster, his mount following his command and heaving higher in the waves.

"He moves as if he were racing." She jiggled about, her gaze on Fedele's churning movement of fore legs and hind legs below the surface. "This is thrilling."

"I'm glad you're enjoying yourself." He steered his mount around the curve of the point where the waves slapped into the craggy rocks spearing out from the headland, then he guided his horse toward the small island up ahead.

"Don't tire, Fedele." Patting him, Olivia leaned over his horse's neck and rubbed her cheek against his silky mane. "There's a good boy. Swim onward."

"Fedele can swim for a mile or two with no issue. I've tested his strength several times along this particular stretch of the coastline and he rises to the challenge each and every time."

"This is delightful." Grasping the pommel, she raised her face to the blue skies above and let out a deliciously decadent sigh. "Thank you for bringing me out for a ride this day, *Amati*."

"I have more than a ride planned for you. Our adventure has just begun." He slid one hand underneath the hem of her cream blouse, her red riding skirts now heavy and wet in the water. Stroking the soft skin of her middle, he murmured in her ear, *"Un momento senza di te è un giorno senza sole."*

"Mmm, I love it when you speak Italian to me." She pushed her skirted bottom back against him. "Please, tell me what you just said."

"A moment without you is a day without sunshine."

"Oh, how deliciously poetic." Eyeing him, she licked her lips, wetting them in the most enticing way, her golden eyes sparkling with stunning brilliance. "I want to kiss my prince."

"You may, as soon as we reach the island. It's completely out of bounds to anyone other than our immediate family. I asked Giovani to deliver a surprise there for us." He steered them toward the curve of white sand surrounded by high cliffs, the cove a sparkling jewel.

"Does the island have a name?"

"It's called *Gioiello del Paradiso*. Jewel of Paradiso."

"How perfect."

"It's also the place where my ancestors first came ashore hundreds of years ago."

"Can we explore it?" She bounced about.

"Absolutely." He slapped the reins, urged his horse toward the island and when Fedele's hooves hit the sandy seafloor, he surged through the surf and galloped onto the beach. Dismounting with a swing of one leg, he landed on the ground then caught Olivia around her waist and lifted her free. Gently, he settled her on the sand and knelt before her. He wrung out the dripping hem of her red riding skirts while she leaned her hands on his shoulders.

"I'm not sure I can walk in these riding boots."

"I'll remove them. Lift one foot." She did and he loosened first one boot then the other. Done, he rose and with her footwear in hand, led her toward the trees.

"You do realize that if my mama ever visits, she'll think I'm a heathen." In her stockinged feet, she walked at his side as he led Fedele toward the stream. "No footwear. No riding hat. I'm half soaked to my skin most of the time."

"You're also perfect, just the way you are." He secured the reins of his mount to the nearest tree bordering the stream and Fedele dunked his snout in and guzzled water.

"Oh my, what pretty flowers." She skipped ahead, knelt and plucked several wildflowers bobbing their colorful heads in the lush grass. "How beautiful."

"Not much farther now." He caught her hand and tugged her through the trees then halted when he reached the blue tartan blanket which he'd asked Giovani to spread, a wicker basket sitting in the center. "Take a look in the basket, *dolce amore mio*."

"We're having a picnic?" Gasping, she lowered to her knees on the blanket, her damp skirts flaring out behind her. She opened the lid of the basket and rummaged within. "It appears the chef has prepared all of our favorite foods."

"Would you like to serve, or shall I?" He lowered and sat beside her.

"Allow me." She grinned at him. "What would you like to eat first?"

"Whatever you wish to feed me." He sprawled out on his back, folded his hands behind his head and smiled as the sun speared through the bright green foliage overhead. The leaves swayed with the softest flutter, the sound of the surf beyond the trees a lulling melody, as was the twitter of the birds up high in their nests.

"Do you remember our first picnic?" Leaning over him with a slice of lean pork in hand, she fed him the meat seasoned with the perfect amount of chili, then nibbled a slice herself.

"*Sì*, in Hyde Park, with Adrestia and Giovani accompanying us." He'd never forget that day.

"I got tossed from my horse during our ride and you caught me." She lowered her lashes, sent him a veiled look before sliding another slice of pork between his lips. "You also took me sailing along the Serpentine after we'd eaten."

"We got saturated from the rough ride."

"Which isn't unlike my current state." She touched her lips to his lips, her breath whispering warmly across the seam of his mouth. "What is the Italian word for freedom?"

"*Libertà*."

"*Libertà, grazie*. Thank you for the freedom you've given me this day, Anteros." She kissed him, long and slow, her lips moving over his with a sweet sizzle of the chili. With one of her hands pressed against his chest, she slowly curled her fingers inward. He went to wrap his arms around her and take control of their kiss, but she suddenly pulled back with an admonishing look. "No, no, no. Let's finish eating before this meal gets forgotten."

"I've already forgotten it."

"I'm sure you have, but I'm eating for two and I'm famished. Let's see what we shall eat next?" With a teasing smile, she lifted a plate of sun-dried tomato bread from the basket and set it beside them. After drizzling olive oil over the bread, she carefully set prosciutto and cheese on top and passed him the sandwich.

They both ate, then devoured the deep-fried Sicilian

rice balls filled with ham and cheese, the dish flavored with a rich pesto sauce. Lastly came dessert, a sweet lemon and peach tart.

Content and full, he smoothed one hand over her flat middle as she laid down beside him, her pregnancy not yet noticeable, although he was well aware she carried his *bambino*. She'd first told him atop the grassy hill near his *castello*, the hilltop overlooking the Bay of Paradiso.

"Anteros?" She suddenly sat up and peered toward the beach. "Did you hear that?"

"All I hear are the birds and the bees and—" He caught a grunt echoing from the beach. He jerked upright too. "No one should be here. Allow me to check."

He pushed to his feet, strode through the trees and halted on the beach.

Up high along the cliffs, a muffled oath sounded from someone who disappeared over the top. Stones skittered down the steep craggy cliff face.

His people knew *Gioiello* was out of bounds, which meant someone else was here, someone who posed a threat. He snarled under his breath. That someone was about to learn exactly why he was called *the cobra*.

Chapter 2: Adrestia

Frustration sizzled through Adrestia as she stood at the helm of her ship and bellowed orders to her crew. "I want more wind in those sails. We can't allow Captain Nazari to elude us."

"Aye, aye, Captain," her men chorused as they worked the rigging with ruthless determination. The sails got heaved higher, the thick canvas catching the wind and sending her vessel skimming across the azure Mediterranean waters.

Holding her telescope to her eye, she searched the small islands dotting the sea. Homes had been built into the surrounding sandstone cliffs, the grassy and craggy terrain leading up to hilly rises. Among those islands were far smaller islands, completely uninhabitable, only bush and scrub able to survive on the rocky land, although each and every one of those islands could be hiding Nazari and his ship from her sight.

How maddening, and why on earth was he trying to

hide from her when they were expecting him? His appearance would be welcome, well not exactly welcome, but at least they wouldn't attempt to blast him out of the water with their cannons before he'd dropped anchor and delivered Shira's plan of attack.

Instead, this morning along Paradiso's coastline, she'd been cruising not far out at sea in wait for him when she'd spied him through her telescope dropping anchor within the cove of *Gioiello del Paradiso*. Shocked, her mouth had dropped open. Nazari knew no one was permitted on that island other than her family.

She'd immediately ordered her crew to change tack and with the barrel of her scope still at her eye, she'd watched him lift his own scope and train it on her. He'd smirked, given her a jaunty wave, then pulled the anchor and cruised back out into the open seas.

So infuriating. Beyond infuriating.

What game did he think to play?

Well, she'd best him in whatever game it was.

She wasn't allowing him to outrun her. Out-hide her either.

"It's time to find our prey," she commanded her crew. "Set the stunsails."

The smaller sails would aid her in gaining extra speed to catch him.

"You heard the captain!" Her first mate clapped young Wills on the back. "Get aloft, lad."

Wills scuttled up the ropes to the highest beam along the mizzenmast.

"Look for the braces, Wills," she hollered up to him. "There can be no tangling of the ropes. Await my

command for release."

"Aye, Cap'n." Wills stretched along the beam, hands at the ready on the ropes, the boy she and Anteros considered family having joined her today on board *The Decadence*.

"Stunsail boom ready," another crewman bellowed.

"Heave ho," she ordered, and Wills sent the stunsails billowing out.

Everyone cheered.

Now she'd evened the playing field.

With her ship skimming the waves at high speed, she navigated around each of the closest islands, the high waves crashing into the bow and sending a salty spray misting over her. She'd find him soon. Hands firm on the wheel, her thoughts returned to the last time she'd come face to face with Nazari. That had been in a tavern near the docks in Lisbon a month past.

She still wanted to wring his neck after their unexpected encounter.

Nazari had caught her arm and steered her into a darkened antechamber, the rowdy crowd of patrons in the main room of the tavern thankfully too far away to see them together. Once he had her alone, he'd whispered in her ear, "Why do you torment me so, little leopardess?"

"I'm sorella del cobra, *sister of the cobra, not your little leopardess." She'd turned on him, pushed him up against the wall where only a sliver of muted light filtered through. "What are you doing in Lisbon?"*

"Wishing to speak to you, of course." With a sensual murmur, he'd whipped them around as she'd done and changed their positions. With his nose touching her nose,

he'd cranked an arrogant eyebrow.

"You can't bend me to your will, Nazari. Release me." She'd heaved one knee, went to slam it into his groin but he countered her move and pinned her knee to the wall instead.

"I would never attempt to, not when your will is unbendable." A carnal smile, his dangerous scent swirling all about her.

"Alessandro Nazari Hazim, release me now." She took a deep, steadying breath before shoving against his chest, which had only made him rock back one inch before pressing against her again.

"When you say my name in that way…ahh, it is musica *to my ears."*

"Why are you following me?"

"I arrived in Lisbon first, which in truth, means you are following me." Another brush of his nose against her nose, the infuriating man far too close for her comfort.

"I'm here to speak to the tavern owner, not you," she'd uttered.

"Word is that you are searching for several pieces of antique jade."

"Do you know something about it?"

"The jade was originally placed on board a ship that sunk across the Atlantic." He spread one hand on the wall beside her head. "The jade belongs to the Portuguese Royal family, which means it could fetch a pretty price should I be the one to find it." He smiled slyly. "And return it to the Royal family."

"The jade has already been thieved once since recovery. I won't allow you to be the second thief."

"Two thieves are better than one. It makes the jade even more valuable."

"You're not getting your hands on it." Gritting her teeth, she'd dropped the dagger sheathed at her wrist into her hand and pressed the pointy tip against his rigid abs. *"I'll never allow it."*

Ignoring her glinting blade, he leaned in with a dangerous tilt to his upper body. "Tesoro mio, mì sono infatuata di te. I'm infatuated with you."

"Now you're truly asking to be gutted." She wouldn't fall for his pretty words.

"I miss you." He blew a soft breath against her neck.

"How does Shira tolerate you?" Still, he persisted, so she pressed her dagger a little deeper, getting incredibly close to breaking his skin.

"We both know you don't wish to hurt me." Eyes darkening, he skimmed one hand down her arm, caressing her with the gentlest touch, then he'd covered her hand and loosened her fierce grip on the hilt of her dagger.

"I'm not one of your doxies, ready and willing to be toppled into your bed."

"That, my leopardess, I'm well aware of." He emitted a low growl before releasing a sensual sigh. *"Truth be told, you are more precious than any doxy I've ever met."*

"You are full of lies."

"It's the truth, Adrestia. You are the light at the end of the tunnel, the sweet taste of freedom, and the heavenly scent of a warm sea breeze leading the way home. You are all those things to me, and so much more."

"Enough. I'll leave you be, if you leave me be." She sheathed her dagger, pushed and thankfully, he eased back

a step.

That was when she noticed what he was wearing. Certainly, not his usual corsair attire. Tonight, he'd dressed in impeccably pressed breeches, his white shirt starched and cravat perfectly knotted, his gold-embroidered waistcoat fitting divinely. Gold cufflinks gleamed from his shirt cuffs, and his boots were so shiny she could almost make out her own reflection in them.

"For what occasion are you so well attired?" She held her position.

"I'm expected at the Braganza's royal residence here in Lisbon." He brushed a stray piece of lint from his shoulder. "I'm about to make an offer for Maria Isabel's hand."

"You can't be serious?"

"I'm more than serious."

"Maria Isabel is a child, not to mention my cousin. I'm also very aware her guardian wouldn't permit a marriage as yet."

"She is sixteen, and her guardian remained here to see her wed before he joins the remainder of the Royal family across the Atlantic within the Portuguese Viceroyalty of Brazil."

"You can't make an offer for her. She still grieves for her parents, and—and—" She had no more arguments. "I forbid it."

"I can understand Maria Isabel's loss better than anyone else. I lost my mother when I was a child, or have you forgotten?"

"Of course not, and you still have your father."

"He is a terrible excuse for a human being."

"So are you. You'll no doubt do the same as him. Fill a harem with women you consider as no more than slaves."

"You know me better than that." Hurt flashed in his eyes.

"I'm sorry." She did, and he didn't deserve such accusations. Which was why she'd brought their encounter to a swift close. She'd turned on her heel and left.

She gave her head a shake and returned to the moment. Rubbing her palms along the smooth wood of her ship's wheel, she searched the crystalline waters for him. It was time to catch *the leopard*. No more could she delay.

Chapter 3

Anteros took a running jump and seized the slit in the craggy rock cliff face.

Swinging upward, he nabbed each hand and foothold and climbed.

Halfway up, he caught the distinct mark on the rock of where the intruder had left their booted scuffmark behind. He was more than ready to throttle this interloper.

"Anteros!" Olivia shouted from below on the beach, her hands cupped to her mouth. "Where are you going?"

"To find out exactly who has dared to step foot on this island." All the residents of Paradiso knew not to trespass on *Gioiello*. It belonged to him and his family alone.

"Perhaps it was Giovani returning for the basket?" She gave him a hopeful look.

"No, he knew I wished for absolute privacy with you this day." He grabbed the next handhold and heaved up. Something fluttered about in a slit in the rock directly above his head. A piece of paper.

He climbed toward it, made the ledge and shuffled along.

Carefully, he plucked the paper from the slit and turned it over. It was sealed with red wax holding the Dey of Algiers' insignia.

"What have you found?" On the tips of her stockinged toes, she peered up at him.

"A message from Dey Hazim." Under his breath, he growled as he broke the seal. After he unfolded the paper, he read out loud, "*La morte viene per la tua sposa.*"

"*Morte.* Isn't that *death*?" Shock vibrated through Olivia's voice.

"*Si.* Death comes for your bride. That is the message Hazim has sent us." He stuffed the message into his pocket, stabbed his fingers into the next handhold and swung higher. Whoever had delivered this message would soon know death themselves. No one, absolutely no one, threatened his wife's life.

"Be careful, Anteros." Olivia searched his gaze. "Please."

"I can't ignore this threat." He grasped the top edge of the cliff, rolled over the precipice and keeping low in a crouch, scanned the cliff top. No one was up here, although a set of boot prints led away. He traced the prints with one finger. They were small, belonged to a child.

"Have you found something?" Olivia called, her voice getting whipped away on the breeze.

"I have." He eased to the edge. At the base of the rock wall, she stood with her hands pressed to the craggy surface. "A set of prints, and they belong to a child."

"Are you certain?"

"I'm certain."

"I don't understand."

"Hazim is known for using children to send messages, children he considers expendable. Slave children."

"That's awful." Disgust flared on her face.

"I need you to take Fedele into the trees and stay out of sight while I find the child. Promise me you'll remain hidden."

"I promise." She clutched her skirts, fingers clenched tight in the red folds. "Don't be long."

"I won't. Now go." He waited as she hurried across to his horse and unknotted the reins. Only once she'd led his mount into the trees and remained hidden from his sight, did he follow the line of prints.

Chapter 4: Nazari

It had taken Nazari far too long to lose Adrestia out at sea. He'd had to leave *Gioiello del Paradiso* and sail around one of the many scattered islands of the Mediterranean before choosing one to remain out of sight behind.

Shira would be pleased, that he'd been able to follow her detailed plan thus far. She'd said he'd have to get his hands dirty in the days to come, which would all begin with the delivery of the missive from Hazim. His father had every intention of stealing Anteros's new bride away, and if he'd declined the task, then Hazim would have sent another to attend to it. That wasn't an option, not for him or for Shira.

Shira's words from prior to his leaving Algiers shimmered though his head. *"Nazari, I need you to look after the lad delivering Hazim's missive, then to sail to where Olivia remains hidden on Gioiello. You won't have long while Anteros searches, and Olivia is an inquisitive sort. She'll wish to learn more about you. Are you prepared for the challenge?"*

"The lady will have only heard unsavory things."

"Olivia doesn't judge people unfairly."

"Why can't I just tell her about your plan, rather than resort to the means of espionage that you've outlined?" Not that he didn't enjoy espionage. Shira knew how often he'd committed such acts against his father.

"The exact details surrounding my plan will go astray if Anteros learns of it. I can't have that happening Do you trust me, Nazari?"

"Of course, I always have and always will."

Shira had been watching over him since the day of his birth, as well as guiding him following his mother's death when he'd been a boy of five. Such a courageously strong mother, he'd had. She'd stood up to his father during the difficult days of her marriage, until the final moments when she no longer could. So many beatings she'd taken. He'd been present in the dungeons when she'd breathed her last. One of the guards had fisted the back of his tunic to keep him standing still while his mother had been strapped to the rack. Once bound with rope, his father had taken his barbed whip and struck her with it.

Thwap, thwap, thwap.

His mother had cried out with each lashing, the skin of her back getting shredded, but she'd still caught his gaze and urged, *"Close your eyes, Alessandro. You do not need to watch this, my son."*

He'd tried to close his eyes as she'd asked, but the guard had slapped his face and demanded he keep them open.

He'd never forget her haunting screams, nor the moment when her head had slumped forward and she'd gone completely quiet. He'd thought her dead, but then she'd whimpered and slowly lifted her head once more.

His father had roared with anger, unsheathed his scimitar and sliced her head clean away.

It had bounced on the floor and landed at his feet, a river of red all around. So much blood. Too much blood.

His heart had torn in two that day, his loss so great, although his mother's strength had also infused him. In that moment, he'd vowed to get his vengeance. A life for a life. His mother deserved the settling of scores. Unfortunately, he'd been far too young to fight.

"Cap'n, land at port bow," the boy in the crows' nest hollered from his high perch.

He set all thoughts of his beloved mother aside.

With his telescope raised to his eye, he found Paradiso.

Time for phase two of Shira's plan—the scheming and devious phase.

He would see it through. He had no choice.

Chapter 5

Olivia stuffed her stockinged feet into her boots and once more paced between the trees as birds chirped overhead and the sea rolled into shore. Worry. It came far too easily to her these days.

"We should see if your master is back yet." She nabbed Fedele's reins which she'd roped to a branch and tugged them free. Hurrying with the stallion trotting after her, she returned to the beach and with one hand raised to her brow, searched the cliff top for any sign of Anteros.

Nothing yet.

She struck a look out to sea and her heart skipped a beat.

A warship crested the swell, the flag flying at the top of the mizzenmast holding the lithe yet savage image of *the leopard*, its fur yellowish-brown patterned with black rosettes. The *Saif.* She'd never seen that ship before, but she knew exactly who it belonged to since Anteros and Adrestia had both described the vessel in great detail to her.

Captain Nazari, it appeared, was about to arrive.

"Anteros!" Clasping her skirts, she jumped for the first handhold, her fingers scraping the stone before she toppled back onto her backside. She pushed to her feet, slapped the sand from her rear and shook out her skirts. She'd mastered tree climbing during her childhood, but she'd never mastered cliff climbing. She'd never even attempted it, and right now she wished she had.

"Shorten the sail. Turn to leeward." At the helm, the man shouting those orders stood with his razor-sharp scimitar sheathed at his hip, his dark hair blowing back in the wind, and his booted feet braced wide apart.

As the ninety-gun vessel dipped down at the bow, the figurehead of a bare-breasted woman got drenched. Water sluiced over her and the massive leopard carved at her feet, its claws digging into the ship's prow.

"Topmen aloft. Prepare to haul in the sails," Nazari commanded loud and clear. "Toss the anchor." Two crewmen heaved the weighty anchor over the side and it disappeared into the sea with a splash and heavy clank of chain. "Take the wheel, Hadid."

"Aye, aye, Captain." The first mate took the wheel.

Nazari bounded down from the helm onto the foredeck.

Not only had he arrived, but it appeared she was about to welcome him to Paradiso. On her own. Something she'd never thought would happen.

"Just remember," she murmured to herself, "this is all part of Shira's plan. We need Nazari if Anteros and I are to survive what's coming for us."

Firming her stance, she stepped across to the edge of

the sea where the surf rolled into shore, Fedele standing guard at her back.

Shira trusted Nazari, which meant he had to have some redeemable qualities, even though Anteros and Adrestia hadn't been able to list any of them to her. With her hands cupped to her mouth, she shouted, "Welcome to Paradiso, Captain Nazari. Come ashore."

"Your Royal Highness." A dip of his head as he swept into a bow near the railing. "We haven't been formally introduced, but please, call me Alessandro."

"We do not know each other well enough for the use of first names."

"That can be remedied." He winked at her, actually winked.

"I'm certain it can't." She shook her head profusely.

"Please, you surely can't fault me for attempting the persuasion. You are a beautiful woman." Grinning, he gave a two-fingered signal to one of his crew, which had the man lowering a skiff over the side and into the swell. Nazari climbed down the roped netting, dropped into the skiff and with the oars in hand, rowed toward her. He caught the rising crest of a wave, cruised into shore and bounded into the knee-deep waves. With his black tunic flapping open all the way to his navel, he hauled his boat up onto the sand and swaggered across to her.

She turned her gaze away from all that golden skin he had showing. Except that might show a weakness and she didn't wish for that. She looked at him again, but kept her gaze pinned above his chin. "Sir, I am a married lady and, ah, I would like you to button your tunic."

"I don't have buttons for this tunic, or at least I did, but two days ago one of the tavern wenches got rather eager upon seeing me and ripped them off before I could ever tumble her to the—"

"Never mind." She waved a dismissive hand. "There is no need to explain."

He grinned again. "Anteros is a lucky devil to have wed such an understanding woman. You are quite ravishing to look upon."

"Speaking of my husband. He is an excellent shot with his pistol."

He boomed with laughter.

"I'm quite serious."

"This is a delightful conversation." He came one step closer. "I'm also well aware of your husband's marksmanship since I've been on the receiving end of more than one of his shots. Thankfully, I've managed to survive thus far."

"You won't survive the next shot."

"I beg to disagree." He raised a staying hand. "Might I also say, his sister is an excellent shot too, a woman I've not long escaped out at sea. This is also the second time I've dropped anchor here this day. I dropped off a lad earlier with a message from my father. Shira instructed me to set the boy ashore here on *Gioiello* so he could deliver it."

"We received that message and why on earth would you try to escape Adrestia? She's been awaiting your arrival with great anticipation. Every day she sails back and forth along the coastline in the hope of sighting your ship."

"Which is the same as saying she's been like a caged animal awaiting her feeding time, me being her next meal."

He motioned to the cliffs. "Paolo is just a boy. He certainly means no harm."

"Why would you bring a child here?"

"Believe it or not, this is all part of Shira's plan." He plucked something from between his two front teeth with one sharply cut nail, then flicked it away. "Of which there will be many facets you mightn't understand."

"Then, please, do enlighten me."

Chapter 6

Methodically, Anteros checked each and every crevice as he searched for any further tracks the child-intruder had left. Hazim was certainly an *idiota* for issuing a threat against his wife, and even more so for sending a child to do his dirty work.

A lone tumbleweed blew past, lifted off the edge of the cliffs and took flight, while along the horizon, a gray tinge darkened the sky. A storm brewed, which meant he didn't have long to find the child before the storm closed in.

A second tumbleweed hit his legs and he nabbed it, snapped off what he needed to forge a makeshift torch and marched across to the entrance into the caves that weaved below these cliffs.

Those caves would make the ideal hiding spot.

He clambered over the rocks and lowered to a crouch at the very edge of the craggy opening. Squinting, he searched the darkened recesses of the cavern far below.

With a strike of his flint against his dagger, a spark

caught and the dry tumbleweed ignited.

Holding the torch in one hand, he swung down into the cavern, his knees bent as he landed. His boots hit the gritty rock beneath his feet and sliding his saber free from his scabbard, he held his position as he waited for his sight to adjust to the darkened interior.

Once it had, he eased one step forward, then a second step. Waving his torch, he circled the perimeter of the cavern looking for any movement within the shadowy corners. No child yet.

Crunching across gritty sand, he searched next for any possible marks of passage, and there, just a few feet ahead, the soft imprint of a boot lay. Lowering to one knee, he measured his own boot print against the print as he'd done above ground when he'd first scaled the cliffs. This print was an identical match to the one above.

Scrubbing a hand across his face, he muttered under his breath.

Which poor child had Hazim sent to deliver his message? Likely one he kept in the slave pens and cared naught about.

Well, Anteros had never harmed a child, and he didn't intend on starting now. Which meant he needed to find this child quickly. Children could be inquisitive beings and even though everyone on this island knew *Gioiello* remained off limits, it still hadn't stopped a child from the nearby village from sneaking over in a skiff. That had been two years past, but the trip hadn't ended well for the young one.

He and Giovani had sailed to this cove and found the missing skiff on the beach. They'd hunted everywhere

before scaling the cliffs and entering these tunnels just as he'd done today. They'd weaved through the passageways, gone as far down into the depths as possible before hitting water. The tide had been high, the deepest recesses covered by the sea. That's when he and Giovani had found the child's body. That wouldn't happen today.

Taking a deep breath, he followed the child's tracks. He skidded in some places where the ground was sludgy and wet, but he kept going. Down, down, down. Water sloshed around his legs, then his hips and—his gut tightened.

"*Ajuda-me!* Help!" A boy's scream echoed off the walls.

He broke into a run.

"I'm coming. *Vindo. Vindo*," he yelled in the same dialect of Portuguese the child had used. He splashed through the strong surge of seawater flooding the tunnel and holding his torch high, the flames licking the low, craggy ceiling, he finally caught sight of the boy up ahead. The lad heaved with the tide swelling about his neck.

He had no time to spare.

He rushed forward, water gushing even higher.

He jammed his torch into a slit in the rock wall close to the ceiling. "Where are you caught? *Onde é que é saqueado?*"

"*O meu pé*. My foot." A gurgle of both Portuguese and English, the boy spitting water as he tried to keep his head above the surface. "Please, my foot is stuck."

"Hold tight." He dived below the water and snagged the boy's trapped foot. A bone protruded from the child's ankle. He heaved and even underwater, the boy's screams rang in his ears. Bones could heal, but a dead child couldn't. Giving the lad's leg another hard yank, he caught the pop as the boy's foot broke free. Leaving the wedged boot behind, he pushed to the surface, scooped the child into his arms and shuddered as the boy's sobs wrenched at his heart. "We need to leave these tunnels, young one. Grab the torch for me. We'll need the light to guide our way."

"It hurts." The boy wiped his face, tears streaming down his cheeks, but he bravely plucked the torch free, gave him a watery smile. "*Obrigado*. You saved me."

"Let's get you out of here." Carrying the boy, he slogged uphill along the tunnel until he reached a side vent which came out along the beach. He took that vent with a quick stride. "There is a doctor on the island. He'll tend to your injury as soon as we get to the castello."

"*Desculpa*." The boy's voice broke. "I am sorry."

"What's your name?"

"P-Paolo, and I w-wasn't the one who wrote the *missiva*. Dey Hazim did."

Water dripped from above and ran down Anteros's face. "Explain, if you will."

"The dey offered me my freedom, but only if I delivered the *missiva* to you. Shira traded readings for the deal. He put me on board the *Saif*."

"Captain Nazari's ship?"

"Yes, and Nazari brought me to this cove and told me to deliver the *missiva*. He asked me to draw you away from the beach for as long as I could. Those were Shira's wishes conveyed to him, and so I obeyed."

"Where did Nazari go after bringing you here?"

"Back out to sea, but he said he would return. Sir,

please..." The boy shivered, his scrawny arms and legs shaking. "Dey Hazim and Barossa have my sister *capturado*. They keep her in the dungeons and they hurt her. Every single night, I hear her screams."

"I'll find her and I'll free her." An easy oath to give. "Your English is impeccable." Which pointed to him being from a household that had the money to ensure his education.

"My father was a professor of languages. He tutored in the homes of the wealthy. We lived in Lisbon, my sister and I, until Captain Barossa invaded our home and killed my parents." He wiped his nose with the wet sleeve of his tattered and torn tunic. "Yakira is the only family I have."

"Is that your sister's name?"

"Yes, sir." The boy glanced ahead and pointed at the muted light filtering through from the opening covered with bushes. "Are we almost free of these tunnels?"

"We are." He pushed through the bushes and stepped into the bright daylight, then lowered the boy onto the grassy ground near the trees not far from where he'd left Olivia, although he didn't see her anywhere. Gently, he eased the remaining boot from Paolo's non-injured foot and set it aside. He touched the area around the boy's bruised ankle where the bone protruded. "Well, it could be worse."

"This injury is naught compared to my sister's injuries." Paolo touched a mottled bruise on his right cheek, one tinged with yellow. "Shira told me about you, stories of your courage. I want to be courageous too."

"Tell me all about those stories while I fashion you a splint." He rose and searched the ground, then snatched two sturdy sticks from near the closest tree, as well as a length of thin, stringy brush to use as roped twine to hold the splint together. He knelt before Paolo, the boy having not yet spoken a word. "Are you all right?"

"I miss my sister." The boy reached and gently touched the protruding bone. "Will it heal?"

"It will in time." He nudged the boy's hand away. "Allow me to strap it, and while I do, tell me how you first met Shira."

"Shira came to the pens where I was being kept with the other children. She brought herbs to heal those of us who were sick, blankets to keep us warm when the nights were cold, and food to fill our bellies."

"You will never return to those pens again." He stripped the sturdy sticks of any sharp edges, placed them either side of Paolo's broken ankle and lower leg and strapped it all together. Looking the boy firmly in the eye, he gripped his chin. "You will stay with me, right here on Paradiso, safe and well. Is that understood?"

"Yes, sir." The boy pushed his wet hair back. "Thank you, sir."

"Come. It's time for you to meet my wife." He snagged a sturdy branch lying close, one long and thick enough to act as a crutch to hold the boy's weight. Propping it under one of the Paolo's arms, he stated, "Try not to injure your foot any more than you already have." He hoisted the boy to his feet. "Right, we've got a short walk ahead of us. Nothing strenuous."

"Shira told me about your wife." The boy sent him a crooked smile. "She said she's an angel."

"Shira's right. My wife is an angel." He grasped the boy's shoulders. "What else did Shira say?"

"She said Nazari would look after your wife while you looked after me."

"Pardon?" His ears rang. "Did you say Nazari is here?"

"I did." The boy pointed through the trees.

Leaving the boy behind, he was off, racing through the copse. He jumped over the small stream trickling into the bay, cleared the shrubbery and skidded onto the beach. There at anchor bobbed Nazari's ship and blast it all, but it was as the boy had said. Nazari was here, and he stood next to Olivia as if he hadn't a care in the world. Marching across, he pulled out his pistol and aimed it at Nazari. "Step away from my wife."

"It's been a long time, Anteros." Nazari slanted his head, gave him one of those infuriating grins he'd always despised. "You look well."

"Don't say—"

"Don't shoot me." Nazari held up his hands as he stared past him toward Paolo currently hopping toward them with his crutch. "What did you do to Paolo?"

"I didn't hurt him. I rescued him after you placed his life in jeopardy."

"Are you all right, lad?" Nazari rushed past him and lowered to one knee in front of Paolo. "What happened to your ankle? Is that a broken bone?"

"I got my foot caught." The boy wobbled about. "I almost drowned."

"Drowned? At the top of the cliffs? That's where you were supposed to go." Nazari gently inspected the splint.

"I found an entrance to the tunnels from up top. I was *curioso*. I weaved down through the passageways until I hit water.”

“You can tell me all about what happened once you’re back on board the *Saif.* I’ll have Hadid take a look at your ankle.”

“You’re not taking the boy with you.” Anteros shoved his pistol back in his pocket. “And Hadid won’t be able to reset that bone. That man knows how to sail a ship exceptionally well, but that’s about it.”

“Hadid has reset every broken bone my crew have ever had,” Nazari muttered as he glared at him. “He’s gotten rather good at it lately. Most of the bones heal fairly straight now.”

“The boy will be tended to by an experienced physician. I won’t have him limping about for the rest of his life. Bring him to my home and when you do, you and I will talk more about why you’ve been frolicking about my beaches dropping off lads when you’re supposed to be bringing me a plan of attack.”

“There was only one lad, and no frolicking whatsoever, but regardless, I agree. We will talk. That’s what Shira has asked.” With a slight inclination of his head, Nazari rose and scooped Paolo up. He remained standing there, looking Anteros in the eye. “I’ll have your word that you won’t blow me out of the water when I arrive.”

“You’ll have the boy on board, so that is guaranteed.”

“Of course.” Nazari gave a snort, understanding crossing his face. “That’ll be the other reason why Shira told me to bring Paolo.”

“I’ll send Giovani to meet you at the wharf. When you see him, come ashore.” As Nazari stalked past him, he halted him with one hand on his shoulder. “The lad will remain here under my care, never returning to Algiers. Am I understood?"

"Shira, I'm sure, would have it no other way." Nazari shook off his hand, crossed to the skiff and seated the boy at the bow. Carefully, he pushed the skiff into the surf, leaped on board and with the oars in hand, heaved through the waves back to his ship.

Anteros kept his gaze on Nazari the entire way, until his nemesis drew in alongside the *Saif* and handed the boy up to Hadid who reached for him. Satisfied all would be well, he pulled Olivia into his arms and murmured in her ear, "If I'd known Nazari was about to arrive, I'd have never left you alone. Did he—"

"I've been more worried about you." She leaned into him as she watched Nazari climb on board himself and take the helm. "Will the boy be all right with Nazari?"

"Nazari, for all his faults, would never actually lay a hand on a child. He suffered too much abuse at his father's hand and would never inflict that kind of torture on another. He'll bring Paolo to the castello. I have no doubt of that."

Across the water, Nazari bellowed orders to his crew. The anchor got pulled. It clanked free of the seabed, while the topmen climbed the rigging and released the sails. From the wheel, Nazari watched the thick canvas rippling with the wind, then the warship cruised out into the open sea. Only once the *Saif* had sailed out of sight did Anteros breathe more easily.

"Nazari said Shira had instructed him to set Paolo ashore to deliver the message on Hazim's behalf." Olivia turned in his arms, slipped her own arms around his waist.

"Shira clearly wanted to get the boy as far away from Algiers as possible. You saving Paolo was all part of Shira's plan."

"I'd agree. She's a clever seer, and as I learned from Paolo, Hazim and Barossa are keeping his sister in their dungeons. I assured the boy I'd find her, which means I must travel to Algiers." He cupped the back of her head, pressed a kiss against her brow. "I'll sort out the finer details once I've spoken to Nazari this eve."

"This is all getting rather complicated." She pressed her hand against his heart.

"Thankfully, I'm used to complicated." He stuffed his hand in his shirt pocket, pulled out the missive Hazim had written and tore it into dozens of pieces which he tossed into the wind. The scraps skittered across the pristine white sand and got swallowed by the surf as it rolled in. "I won't let Hazim lay a hand on you."

"I know you won't."

"I'm also going to make Hazim pay for those words he wrote." Along the seaward horizon, the clouds grew darker and heavier. "A storm is closing in."

"We should leave."

"*Sì*, we should." He caught Olivia around the waist and boosted her into Fedele's saddle, then he swung up behind her and only once he had her nestled protectively within the circle of his arms, did he snap the reins and gallop back along the shore and into the waves. "This eve, we'll learn all the details surrounding Shira's plan of attack. We'll get the information out of Nazari."

"And then?"

"We take her advice under consideration." He pushed

his mount faster, until Fedele swam around the curve of the cove. With another nudge of his knees, he steered them back toward the mainland's beach.

"What caused your friendship with Nazari to splinter apart?" She angled her body toward his, touched her lips to his ear and blew a soft breath against his lobe.

"He betrayed me, showed me that the apple doesn't truly fall far from the tree." He urged his stallion up onto the beach and galloped into the forest. "*Cara,* danger swarms around Nazari. It always has and always will."

"Danger swarms around you too."

"You don't need to remind me of that." In the beginning, he'd fought so hard not to involve her in his life, but she'd been an angel, a bright beacon of light in his dark and dismal world. It had been impossible to stay away from her. "You're so sweet and innocent and trusting. That is your nature, *Amore,* which Nazari will attempt to take advantage of."

"I'm also feisty and strong and a good judge of character."

"You also lead with your heart and not with your head."

"Sometimes leading that way is the better choice."

"I disagree." Although, he was mightily glad she'd chosen to lead with her heart when it had come to choosing him. "I should have tried harder to give you up."

"Except I had already chosen you," she returned with a soft smile. "I will never alter that choice."

"Except you didn't choose the death threats we've currently received. Hazim is a ruthless man, *mio angelo.*"

"You can be rather ruthless yourself."

"I'm about to get even more ruthless, because I'm going to kill Hazim. It's the only way to protect all that I hold dear, you, our unborn *bambino*. I can't gamble all of that away."

"We have a seer on our side." She nuzzled her nose against his neck, the clouds getting thicker and darker with each minute that passed. "Ride faster or else we're both going to get even wetter than we currently are."

"As you wish." He tucked his head over hers and nudged his horse. "I'm yours to command."

He always had been, and always would be.

Chapter 7

Damp skirts slapping against her legs, Olivia bounced in Anteros's lap, the trees rushing by either side of the forested trail as they galloped toward home. Fallen leaves swirled in small eddies behind them, while overhead the skies got darker, the air getting heavier with the threat of rain.

As a child, she'd always adored getting wet, often stamping through puddles or pestering Papa to take her swimming in the lake near their country estate. Papa had been the one to teach her how to swim and dive and frolic and play in the water, while Mama would watch on from where she sat on the shore with a book usually in hand.

Anteros rubbed her arms. "*Sei freddo.* You're shivering."

"I'm cold, but that's naught that a lovely hot bath won't remedy."

"We're almost home." He bolted out of the forest and raced along the grassy verge of the bay. Wild waves surged into the wooden pilings of the wharf and sent seawater slapping over the walkway where two men pushed a trolley loaded with crates toward a ship moored along the jetty. The men got drenched, one losing the cap on his head as the waves stole it away.

Directly around the other side of the bay *La Rocca Dinastia* stood tall and strong, the castello built of thick slabs of tawny-colored stone that rose high on the blustery point overlooking the sea. From the top of each turret, the distinctive gold and sapphire colors of Anteros's cobra flag flew high, while along the battlements his armed men kept an alert eye on the Mediterranean.

Anteros raised a hand to signal the guardsman in the gatehouse and they rode through the stone-arched entrance gate into the inner courtyard. Anteros drew his stallion to a halt before Giovani who awaited them near the marble steps leading up to the wide front doors. Slinging one leg over the side of his steed, Anteros jumped to the paved stones. He landed with a *thump*, grasped her waist and lifted her free of the saddle. Gently, he set her on her feet before handing the reins to a stable hand who rushed forward to take them.

"Ensure Fedele is well fed and brushed down," he instructed the lad.

"Will do, sir." The hand dipped his head before leading the horse away, one of his suspenders swinging loose over his shoulder.

"How was your afternoon?" Giovani asked in a low drawl as he joined them, his black riding breeches tucked into knee-length boots polished to a high sheen. "I've not long returned from a ride myself. It's fortunate you've

arrived home before the rain falls."

"We've had an interesting day. Nazari appeared at *Gioiello*." Anteros clasped Giovani's shoulder then continued to detail all that had occurred, including the death threat, information about the boy who'd delivered that message, and that he'd given Nazari permission to come ashore later this eve with the child. "I'd like you to collect Nazari from his ship and to personally escort the boy, Paolo, to the castello. The child is now under my protection."

"Of course. I'll ensure additional guardsmen are posted around the bay to keep a close eye on Nazari's crew." Giovani took Olivia's hand and pressed a kiss against her knuckles. "*Mie scuse*. My apologies for the disruption Nazari has caused to your day at the cove. I should have stood guard somewhere close by."

"No one knew that's where he'd drop anchor. It appears we have very little sway over Shira's plan."

"You've already come to understand Shira rather well." With a respectful dip of his head, Giovani backed away then turned and strode toward the gatehouse, the wind rising and blowing his dark hair about his shoulders.

She shivered as a chill took her, her clothes still damp.

"I believe that hot bath is now in order." With his hand at the small of her back, Anteros steered her through the front door held open by their elderly butler attired in a black jacket and trousers, his gray head bowed and wire-rimmed spectacles sliding down to the tip of his thin nose.

"Don't lose your glasses, Renzo." Anteros caught them before they hit the tiled floor. He tipped his butler's chin up and plunked his spectacles back on his nose.

"*Grazie*. I'm most fortunate you have quick reflexes, Your Royal Highness." Renzo dipped his head again, almost lost them a second time before pressing them back onto his nose.

"Renzo, I'd like you to organise a meal to be delivered to my private sitting room in an hour, and secondly, I need you to ask one of the runners to fetch the doctor from the village. There's a boy arriving at dusk with Giovani who has a broken ankle. After the doctor has tended to the lad, ensure the boy is given a room next to Wills' chamber. The two of them are of a similar age. Is Wills still out at sea with my sister?"

"He is, sir."

"Send me a message when she returns." Anteros steered her away, her red riding skirts leaving a wet streak on the diagonal black and white tiled floor.

Through the foyer, they walked, then into the grand hall.

She strode past the candles flickering from the wall sconces, the gentle yellow glow flaring out over the low marble columns holding finely carved marble busts. Stunning artwork set in intricate gilt-edged frames hung on the walls, the ceilings above painted by renowned Italian artists, the creation a collage that surely rivaled the Sistine Chapel. In fact, the first time she'd ever stood in this grand hall she'd lost her breath and struggled to regain it. Sometimes, she even reclined on the red leather chaise longue in the center of the hall just so she could lie back and truly enjoy the beauty surrounding her.

No time for that today though.

Anteros swept her up the marble staircase. He guided

her along the upper landing where large stained-glass windows cast a shimmering burst of vibrant colors across the floor.

She walked along the corridor toward their wing and stepped into their bathing chamber, which was by far the largest and most stunning bathing chamber she'd ever beheld. Steamy water was piped up from a deep underground reservoir and filled the large pool carved from marble. It held inbuilt steps and columns rising from all four corners to the high ceiling. The air was warm and sultry. She grasped the waistband of her red riding skirts, removed her outer clothing and in her undergarments, walked up the marble steps warmed from the heat of the chamber.

Anteros stowed his weapons on a marble shelf built into one wall, removed his boots and breeches and in his tunic which swayed to mid-thigh, walked toward her with his gold medallion dangling from the thick gold chain around his neck. He joined her on the top step and she wrapped one hand around the pendant holding his cobra insignia and whispered, "I won't lose you to Hazim."

"I won't lose you either."

"We remain together throughout the difficult days to come." She released his medallion, pressed a kiss against his chin then nibbled along his delectable jaw until she tugged lightly on his lower lip with her teeth. There was nothing more thrilling than being able to touch him as freely as she currently did.

"Pool, now," he uttered and scooped her into his arms. Holding her, he trod down the steps into the pool.

She released a long, heartfelt sigh as he moved through

the heated water with her. The delicious water flowed like silk over her chilled skin. Absolutely wondrous.

Anteros eased down onto the seat rimming the inside of the pool, his big hands settling on her hips as he positioned her on his lap so she faced him.

She luxuriated in his strength and warmth, curled her fingers into his firm shoulder muscles. "Hmm, I'm curious about Nazari's mother. Who was she?"

"Lady Anna Gianna Romano, the daughter of an Italian nobleman and a lady-in-waiting for my mother at the Royal Palace in Palermo."

"Oh, I didn't expect that answer. How did they first meet?"

"In Sicily." He caressed up and down her back. "From time to time, my father extended invitations to Hazim, asking him to join him in Palermo. During one such visit, Lady Anna fell for Hazim's charms. Of course it's hard to believe he had any, but apparently he did." He shifted his hold, one hand still on her back as he moved the other over her belly to where their child lay.

"Did she love him?"

"Let's just say Nazari was born nine months following their first meeting, and if there was any love involved, it certainly soured when she realized she was naught more than a brood mare."

"Lady Anna must have wished to return home."

"None of the women within Hazim's harem have ever escaped it, other than by way of death."

"Does Nazari have a harem?"

"He has yet to take his first wife, although he was in negotiations with the Braganza dynasty for the hand of

Maria Isabel, a young cousin of mine. Adrestia asked me to step in and halt any proceedings, which I successfully managed to do."

"Did that anger Nazari?"

"I hope so." A teasing smile as he gently, reverently, lifted the locket at her neck and slowly rubbed his thumb along the engraving of his mark etched upon it.

"You seem to take pleasure in angering Nazari." Which she couldn't help but say with a naughty smile. "You are altogether far too wicked, *Amati*."

"You've barely even had a taste of my wickedness, *Amore*."

"Then by all means, do show me. We are finally all alone." Which was exactly what her wicked husband did. Anteros was her entire world, and keeping her gaze locked with his, she allowed him to sweep her away to another place and time.

Chapter 8: Nazari

Wind swept through with a misty rain as Nazari prowled to the edge of the slick upper deck. He'd sailed back and forth along the coastline in full view of the castello's guardsmen until he'd sighted Giovani striding down to the wharf. That could only mean they awaited his arrival. Assured of it, he returned to the wheel, relieved his first mate and bellowed to his crew, "To shore, we go!"

His crew battled the high waves, the topside bustling as his men hauled on the ropes and ensured their sails remained full of the wind. As the wharf jutting out from the bay drew closer, he ordered the sails lowered, the anchor dropped. They slowed upon approach, the anchor's chain clanking as it unraveled into the sea. He adjusted the wheel and brought his ship to a crawl alongside the jetty.

Four of his men bounded over the side of the ship, their boots hitting the wooden wharf with a *thump*. They hooked ropes to the supports, the foamy waves rocking them gently against their mooring. They had arrived.

"The exact details surrounding my plan will go astray if Anteros catches wind of it, and I can't have that happening." Shira's last words whispered through his mind. *"Hold fast to your trust in me, Nazari."*

He'd always trusted Shira, from the moment she'd rescued him from the hellhole that had become his home following the brutal death of his sweet mother. So young, he'd been at the time. None of his father's other wives or concubines had ever conceived a child, other than for the nomadic woman who'd given birth to his half-brother, Barossa, in the desert. She'd arrived at the palace carrying her newborn baby wrapped in linens. Hazim had welcomed her, a child born with a witch's aid through a tribal ritual, the mother of that child having left within days so she might return to where she'd come.

He shook his head, brought his thoughts back to the present. It was time to begin phase three of Shira's plan. He strode to the side of his ship where his men had already lowered a plank to the dock.

Giovani thumped along the walkway toward him in black breeches and a coat, his collar flicked up against the wind. "Well, well, if it isn't Captain Nazari Hazim. I never thought I'd see the day when you sailed merrily into this bay without first being shot out of the water."

"I'm as surprised as you, Giovani. I thank you for coming to greet me." He strode down the plank and joined Anteros's right-hand man on the jetty. "My men would like to stretch their legs. May they go ashore?"

"They may, provided they don't venture any farther than the beach." Giovani lobbed a look at his crew, glanced back at him. "I'm here to escort you to *La Rocca Dinastia.*

You're to bring the boy with you. Anteros told me his name is Paolo."

"Paolo is ready and waiting." He gestured to his first mate who stood next to Paolo with one hand on the boy's shoulder. Ali Hadid scooped Paolo up, his makeshift crutch and all, and carried the boy down the slatted board before setting him on his feet on the walkway and propping the crutch back under Paolo's arm. Hadid had taken a look at the boy's broken ankle, re-strapped it as best as he could, then left the injury to be tended to by Anteros's physician.

"It looks as if you might get blown out of the water after all." With a cocky smile lifting his lips, Giovani motioned out to sea and when Nazari followed Giovani's gaze, he saw exactly why the man had uttered those words.

A ship approached with Adrestia standing at the helm.

"Lower the sails," she yelled to her crew from the wheel, her voice echoing across the waves. "Toss the anchor."

It sank into the sea and she slowed and brought her ship into the berth directly across from him. Glaring daggers, she jumped onto the foredeck in a pair of tan breeches and black knee-high boots, her black hair held at her nape with a strip of leather and a thick ruby woolen coat flapping about her ankles.

With one hand gripping the hilt of her side-belted saber, she appeared a fierce vision.

Buttoning his black jacket against the wind trying to tear it off his shoulders, he braced himself as she bounded over the rail, dropped onto the walkway beside him and rose from a crouch.

"You are not, and never will be," she pronounced

precisely, "permitted to drop anchor at *Gioiello*."

"*Tesoro mio, a*s always it is a pleasure to see—"

She pulled back one fist and slammed it into his gut.

"—you." He grunted and stumbled back, clutching his middle while Giovani boomed with laughter.

Arching a brow, he went to speak to her again but she pulled back her other fist.

"Wait." Hands up, he muttered, "There is a child present. You're scaring him." She cast a look at Paolo who was currently smiling just as widely as Giovani so he thumped the boy on the shoulder and growled, "Look scared, lad."

"It's you who should look scared." Adrestia threw another punch.

Chapter 9

Later that evening after he'd bathed and eaten his evening meal with Olivia in their private sitting room, Anteros remained at the table in his rich sapphire silk banyan, his wife having left only a few minutes ago to dress for the evening in her adjacent dressing room, her maid aiding her. Out his window, the skies had begun to darken to a purple hue that reflected the same streaks of purple color across the choppy waves of the sea.

On nearly silent feet, his valet of fifteen years, Rafiq, stepped toward him attired in a blue caftan from his Moroccan homeland. "I bring a message from Renzo, sir. Princess Adrestia has returned. I then spoke to her personally, and she informed me of her news, that she personally welcomed Captain Nazari at the wharf, with a solid exchange of her fists." The proud look in Rafiq's eyes was unmistakable. "She is also aware of your coming meeting with Nazari, would like to attend if she may, but first would like to change for the evening. May I tell her your answer?"

"*Sì*. Tell her to meet me in my study when she is ready. That is where the meeting shall take place." He couldn't help but grin. "*Sorella del cobra* lives up to her name, hmm?"

"You have taught her well, sir." Respectfully dipping his head, Rafiq asked, "Did you enjoy your meal?"

"It was *delizioso*. The duchess particularly enjoyed the gelato. She said it was sweet and creamy, not that I could pry the bowl from her fingers to confirm her findings." He'd managed only a swipe of one finger through the gelato as Olivia had held the dish beyond his reach, and even then she'd licked his finger before he could. His wife had managed to consume all four scoops, two of which should have rightfully been his. "Next time bring eight scoops. Hopefully then I might be able to sneak some from her. Her cravings worsen."

A chuckle escaped Rafiq. "Four children, my delightful Aliyah has given me and while carrying them, she experienced many cravings, gelato being a particular favorite. You'll discover your duchess will crave all manner of sweet, salty, sour, and spicy foods over the months ahead."

"If that is the case, then I need you to ask the chef to keep the pantry and icebox well stocked with all the foods you believe my wife will crave. Double or even triple the stocked items. I have much to learn, and you appear to be the master, Rafiq."

"Simply ask if you would like me to convey any of my vast knowledge. I'm at your service." Rafiq lifted the tray from the table.

"*Eccellente*. After you've seen to that tray, please bring my shaving utensils to my chamber. I am dallying and shouldn't be." He rose from the table and walked into his adjacent bedchamber, crossed to his drinks' table and poured himself a finger of liquid from the crystal decanter.

At his fireplace, he rested one hand on his oak mantelpiece and eyed the crackling flames of the fire licking at the logs. His meeting tonight with Nazari would aid him in being fully prepared for Hazim's coming strike, and the sooner Nazari spoke of Shira's plan, the better. He certainly couldn't allow the threat to his or Olivia's safety to continue.

"I have your utensils." Rafiq returned and set them on the side table before his upholstered armchair. After taking his seat where Rafiq usually shaved him, he held still as his man laid a cloth at his neck and dabbed the lower half of his face with a hot compress to soften his stubble. Once done, Rafiq dipped the shaving brush into the basin of water, foamed the bar of soap then smeared the bubbles across his jaw. Carefully, his valet scraped the blade from his ear to his chin, then followed the path down his neck, swiped under his nose and once done, dabbed the remaining suds with a cloth.

Rafiq collected a freshly laundered shirt and tan breeches from the top drawer of his dresser and aided him in dressing. His man added the finishing touches, knotting an impeccably pressed snowy white cravat at his neck and sliding gold cufflinks in place.

Weapons next. Rafiq gathered them from his trunk nestled against one wall.

He accepted them from his valet, strapped his sword

belt at his waist and crouched to slot his ankle dagger into the leather sheath he kept tucked inside his Hessian boots. After sliding his arms into the sleeves of his black jacket, he said to his valet, "Ask Renzo to escort Nazari to my study as soon as he arrives at our front door. That will be all for the night."

"I shall do so right away, sir. Enjoy your evening."

"That might be impossible with Nazari in my home, but I shall try." Anteros stepped out of his chamber and hands fisted, strode down the passageway and followed the curve of the landing to his study.

He strode through the doorway, his study window across the other side of the room showing the darkness of the night as well as a misting of rain on the glass pane, the wind outside howling.

At his chunky oak desk, he pushed a pile of papers to one side and sat in his leather chair, pressed his elbows to his desktop and steepled his fingers together.

A quick scan showed no papers of importance remained out for prying eyes. He certainly had to take all care when entertaining his enemy, even though his current enemy had been sent by Shira.

Footsteps echoed along the landing and his butler entered, gave a short bow then gestured toward Nazari who strode in directly behind him. "Your Royal Highness. May I present Captain Nazari?"

"You may," he issued before resting back in his chair as his butler discreetly left. "Welcome to my home, Nazari. Do sit."

"Only if you set your dagger aside." Nazari cranked a brow.

"Pardon?"

"The one currently in your hand." The corsair pointed at it.

"My hand?" He stared at his hand, the dagger which had been lying between two piles of papers now firmly in his grip. With a smirk, he flipped it high and caught it by the hilt. "Well, isn't that interesting. I wasn't even aware I'd reached for it."

"You did so the second I walked in the door." Nazari wandered past the crackling fireplace with its oak mantelpiece carved with ornate scrollwork. The corsair eyed the matching oak bookshelves holding leather tomes standing along one wall, then meandered across to it. He tipped one tome out, opened the book and flicked through a few pages before slotting it away again. Across the room, Nazari continued to roam in his black jacket and gray breeches holding damp splotches from the rain, until he finally halted before his window. Slowly, Nazari turned and looked at him. "I had a delightful chat with your sister when she returned from sea, right there on the wharf with Giovani watching on."

"I heard she used her fists."

"Your sister does throw a hard punch, unlike any other lady I've ever met." His adversary propped his backside on the white-painted windowsill, stretched out his legs. "Adrestia's clearly angry that Shira asked me to come. I understand that."

"I'd say she's more angry that you escaped her out at sea earlier this day."

"There is that too."

"Perhaps you should begin speaking of Shira's plan."

He flipped the dagger again. "That might keep you out of trouble for a while."

"I'm certain it wouldn't." A flicker of unease swirled in the corsair's eyes, a long silence drawing out between them before Nazari continued, "If I don't follow Shira's plan of attack exactly as she's detailed then all will be lost. I need you to understand that."

"I understand."

"Good." Crossing one booted foot over the other, the gold-hooped earring adorning his right ear catching in the firelight, Nazari eyed him speculatively. "Shira wishes for us to set our current differences aside so we can work together to take down my father."

"We were friends once, will never be friends again, but I will work with you to eliminate your father. Why is it you still haven't eliminated him on your own?"

"I've tried, or I should say attempted to try." He flexed one fist, stared at his whitened knuckles and loosened his tight grip. "It's hard to explain, Anteros."

"Try. I'm listening."

"Whenever I want to end his life, my mother appears before me. I'm aware this world would be a better place without him in it, but in taking his life, I fear that would make me the same as him." Agitated, Nazari stepped across to the fire and rested one hand on the mantel. "Whereas you are *the cobra*, and no one strikes as swiftly and decisively as you do. You wouldn't still your hand, not as I would."

"Good evening, Captain Nazari." Olivia swept through the doorway, his wife a vision dressed in yellow lace over cream silk, her gown's bodice cinched above her waist and her full skirts flaring out with a short train at the back.

"Come here, *mio angelo*." He rose and held out his desk chair for her. She sashayed across and once seated, he tucked her in and stepped behind her, rested his hands on her shoulders and pressed a kiss to the top of her head. "You look ravishing as always."

"Thank you, *Amati*." She stared up at him, laid one of her hands over his with a sultry smile.

"*Fratello*, have you already begun your conversation with the scourge of the sea?" Adrestia marched in wearing a white blouse and cerulean blue skirts flaring from her waist, a ribbon of the same blue color woven through her midnight-black hair which swayed wild and free down her back.

"We've barely begun, *Sorella*." He tossed Adrestia his dagger which she deftly caught. "Feel free to use this on our guest should you have need of it."

"*Grazie*." His sister didn't miss a step as she continued directly toward Nazari and pressed the tip of the dagger against his neck. "Ahh, I already have need of it. How interesting this night shall be?"

"Your claws are getting sharper and sharper by the hour." Slowly, with leopardlike grace, Nazari curled one hand around Adrestia's on the hilt and leaned in. "Now you're here, it's time I speak about Shira's plan in more detail and depth."

"That is a wise move." Adrestia took a step back. "Proceed."

"*Sì*, proceed. We're ready to hear what you have to say, Nazari." Anteros weaved around his desk and stood side by side with his sister. "Begin."

"Well, there are several steps in Shira's plan, phases as

such."

"What are her steps or phases for me?" Anteros asked.

"On the morrow, you and Adrestia and Giovani will board *The Cobra* and set sail for Algiers. I'll be sailing ahead of you, leaving later this eve, on the high tide." His nemesis stroked his chin, one thumb tapping the deep cleft in the center. "Once you reach Algiers, you'll leave Adrestia on board your ship, keeping it anchored out of sight of my father's guardsmen, then you'll rendezvous with me inside my father's palace, the receiving hall. That is where I'll be awaiting you."

"Shira expects me to walk blindly into your father's stronghold?" That, he hadn't expected.

"You're aware of all the ways to get into the palace. Shira's instructions are that you think back to when your grandfather first brought you to Algiers. He showed you some of the tunnel entrances. She wishes for you to choose one of those passageways in, and to not divulge to me exactly which one."

"I understand." No one else would know his coming route, other than him.

"Good." Nazari lobbed his gaze to Olivia. "You, my dear lady, have a message from Shira too. Do you remember when you first visited her for a reading and she told you that your life had reached a fork in the road?"

"I'll never forget that reading." Her golden eyes brightened.

"At that time, you chose the pathway to your *emir* and learned that his fate was already sealed and remained in your hands. That has not changed, nor has the fact that you must continue to spread your wings and fly."

"Where am I to fly to?" Olivia rose from Anteros's desk chair, crossed to him and stood at his side as she faced Nazari.

"To the second fork in the road," Nazari continued. "Take the path that leads to rescue and release. For that is the only path that Shira watches over us all, always and forever. Shira said you won't understand these words right now, but you will in time."

"All right." She frowned, glanced at him. "What do you think of Shira's message, Anteros?"

"Shira is aware I'd never allow you to leave Paradiso. You are not taking flight anywhere, so keep your wings tucked in." He nestled her closer into his side as he eyed Nazari. "Do you have anything more to add?"

"I do. Shira said Hazim is strong, but his house has always been divided. Barossa stands on one side of that divide, while I stand on the other. As you're aware, there has never been a moment of harmony between us, and it will remain that way until my father pays for his misdeeds. Each and every one of them." Nazari angled his head. "Anteros, you must make him pay."

Such intense emotions flickered in Nazari's eyes, emotions Anteros couldn't ignore or deny. "A life for a life. That is the payment you desire?"

"*Sì*, I made a vow to my mother the night she died. A life for a life. She deserves the settling of scores." Nazari extended his hand. "Will you do me that honor?"

"I will." He clasped Nazari's hand and shook. "To our momentary truce."

"To our momentary truce," Nazari repeated.

Chapter 10

Nazari's last words continued to echo through Olivia's head as she readied for bed later that night after Anteros had escorted Nazari back to his vessel. Tying the sash of her lavender robe at her waist, she paced back and forth in front of the warmth of the fire as Anteros collected a pistol from the top drawer of his bedside table and tucked it down the front of his tan rawhide breeches, adding it to the arsenal he already carried on his body. "Must you leave this night?"

"Giovani and I have a standing assignment to ride to each of the guard-stations positioned around the coastline of Paradiso and ensure each and every hole in our defenses are plugged. No one will be permitted to breach our safe haven. I also need to speak to each of the watchpoint guards before I depart, which must be tonight since I'm leaving on the morrow, as per Shira's plan. Algiers, and the settling of scores, awaits." Tugging on the cuffs of his jacket, he came around the bed and closed the distance between them. "By tomorrow eve, I'll be rendezvousing with Nazari inside Hazim's palace."

"Promise me you'll be careful." She slid her arms around his middle, settled her head on his chest.

"Shira wouldn't have come up with this plan if she hadn't intended for it to work." His deep voice rumbled under her cheek.

"There are a number of obstacles you must still overcome."

"I'm aware." Tenderly, he brushed a lock of her hair behind one ear. "I've been in worst situations."

"If you're intending on calming my nerves, you're doing a terrible job of it." Tipping her gaze to his, she wriggled her bare toes into the plush cream carpet. "I want to come with you. I could stay below deck while you sneak into the palace. Adrestia will never allow any harm to come to me."

"You're staying right here behind these fortified walls."

"But—"

"No buts. This is where you're safest, and where you'll stay." He stroked one finger under her chin, drew her tighter against him with his arm around her waist.

"Is there anything I can say or do to change your mind?"

"I would be a fool to take you and our unborn child into our enemy's territory. If Hazim ever got his greedy hands on you, I would—" He halted, his voice getting brutally hard. "Rather than just kill him, I'd have him drawn and quartered, his body torn into four pieces and hung about his city for the scavenger birds to peck at. I may still do that to ensure Nazari has had his full vengeance."

"For the first time, I can actually imagine how you two might have been friends in the past."

"We think much alike, and we always shall. I've also never professed to being a gentleman. You're aware of my true nature." He tapped her nose. "Give me your word you'll remain here."

"I'll remain here." She gave a consigning nod, trailed her fingertips back and forth across his smooth jaw, the cobra medallion at his neck glinting in the firelight where it lay nestled in the folds of his cravat. "Nazari seems to have many sides to him. When I first met him, he matched the man you'd portrayed him to be, but tonight I also saw a more vulnerable side to him. He's been holding onto a lot of pain."

"Try not to be fooled by him, *Amore*. He has hunted and raided the same as any of Hazim's other corsairs have. He has inflicted pain on others. He is not an innocent man."

"One could say you hunt and inflict pain on others too, albeit with far more honor guiding your decisions and your hand."

"It sounds as if you wish to save him?"

"Doesn't everyone deserve a chance at being saved?"

"Ordinarily, I'd say yes, but in Nazari's case, it's a resounding no. Now," he uttered as he scooped her into his arms. "The hour is getting late and it's time I left. To bed with you."

He carried her to their four-poster bed with its sapphire canopy sweeping down the carved posts and laid her on the richly appointed sapphire covers emblazoned with his golden cobra emblem. Planting his hands either side of her head, he leaned in and bit her lower lip before soothing his bite with a series of hot licks and kisses.

"One day," he murmured as he lifted his head and searched her gaze, "I will show you how exotic the souk of Algiers is, and how magical the desert sands surrounding the city are, but for now, you must remain here on Paradiso where you are safe and well."

"It sounds like a dangerously enchanting place. I'm going to hold you to that promise." She certainly wished to see all he spoke of. She pushed her fingers deep into his silky black hair lit a sizzling blue on the ends by the light of the fire and smiled at him. "Ride swiftly, *Amati*. I shall await your return in the morn. We will spend some time together right here in this bed before you set sail. Are we agreed?"

"We are most certainly agreed, and sleep well, my love." He stepped back, blew out the candles and slipped out of their chamber.

He was gone, although never gone far from her heart.

That is where she held him close at all times.

Chapter 11: Nazari

Nazari had been escorted back to his ship by Anteros immediately after his meeting with him, but that wasn't where he'd remained. No, Nazari had lowered a skiff over the seaward side of the *Saif* and ordered his crew to be ready to set sail the moment he returned. He had a rendezvous with a lady who was about to spread her wings and fly.

Wearing dark robes over his clothes and a black headdress veiling his face, he rowed to the place Shira had marked on a map along the coastline where he needed to make landfall. The fourth phase of her plan had begun. The deadliest phase.

With another glance over his shoulder to ensure none of Anteros's guardsmen had sighted him from the beach or the battlements, he turned the oars a touch and braced himself to beach the skiff along the rocky shoreline on the other side of the castello. Shira had told him that to save Olivia's life, he must first place it in jeopardy. Thus, why he considered this the deadliest phase.

He was about to poke *the cobra.*

Skiff beached, he bounded over the slick black rocks and crept toward the bushes covering the entrance to the tunnel Shira had told him was here. Cutting away the overgrowth with his saber, he thinned what he needed to then squeezed inside the passageway and followed the tunnel into the darkened depths with a torch he'd brought and lit with his flint. Flames flickering over the stone and dirt walls, he held the light high as he set one foot in front of the other.

Massive cobwebs hung from ceiling to floor. He swiped at them as he turned and headed upward, the ground getting firmer. He must be close to his destination.

Up ahead, the tunnel finally opened out into a cavern, a dusty stone door appearing on the far side of it out of the gloom.

"I'm here, Shira," he uttered to himself as he wiped more cobwebs stringing in front of him, her instructions ricocheting inside his head.

She'd told him to stand directly in front of the door. Move two paces back, four to the left, then to lower to his hands and knees. He did exactly that.

Carefully, he patted the packed ground where he knelt, the stones under his feet holding firm, all except for one. He jiggled the large stone loose and waited as cockroaches skittered away.

That's when he found the old iron key Shira had told him about.

It was corroded and caked in dirt. He wriggled it loose, wiped it clean on his breeches and got back on his feet.

At the door, he searched the wall to the left and found a rusty slot the key was supposed to fit into. Not a chance at the moment due to the muck wedged in it. He removed his wrist dagger from its sheath and gently worked the mess free with one careful poke after another.

Shira had said this escape tunnel hadn't been used in over fifty years, that she knew of its existence because Mario had shown it to her once, and when she'd seen it in her reading done for Anteros, she'd known it would come into play during the undertaking of her plan.

Obviously, no one had been down here in an eon. Well, except for that bat hanging upside down within the far shadowy corner, its beady eyes glowing and wings tucked in tight.

He kept working to clear the slot, poking and prodding with his blade until he finally cleared enough of the mess to give the key another go in the slot. He pushed the key in with a grating scrape, gave it another turn and—*click.*

Wonder of wonders. It had worked.

With one shoulder braced against the door, he pushed and the heavy wood scraped eerily open. He returned the key to its hiding place, slipped through the open door and weaved along another dark and dank passageway coated in more cobwebs.

When he reached another door—this one made of marble—he pushed and pushed until it finally gave way.

He snuck inside a bathing chamber housing a large pool, the door he'd entered slotting back into the wall as he closed it. If he hadn't opened the door, he wouldn't have guessed there was one even there, not when it appeared a seamless wall made of marble. How many other such secret passageways were there? Old castles such as this one must hold many.

Carefully, he crept around the edge of the chamber, set his torch in the wall holder near the door and passed into the next passageway. From his pocket, he removed a small bottle Shira had given him, uncorked it and poured some of the belladonna into his handkerchief. The stringent scent of the sedative permeated the air.

He slunk toward the next door in Anteros's private wing, opened it and waited for his eyesight to adjust.

In the near dark, he caught the outline of a canopied bed.

One step closer and the floorboard creaked.

"Anteros?" A sleepy murmur, a shadowy form pushing upright onto elbows thrust into the mattress.

He didn't hesitate.

Shira said he shouldn't.

Shoving the cloth over Olivia's nose and mouth, he held it tightly to her face.

She gagged, let out a muffled cry and slumped.

Chapter 12

With Giovani's aid, Anteros heaved the thick trunk of a fallen tree blocking the forested trail and rolled it out of the way. The trunk got smothered by the dense brush when it rolled into it. Straightening and rolling his shoulders, he wiped his sweaty brow with his handkerchief. "That'll ensure any oncoming riders don't fall prey to this trunk as we almost did."

"That waylaid us for far too long." In his riding jacket and breeches, Giovani brushed his hands against his legs.

"At least we've seen each of the watchmen and relayed the information we needed to."

"True." His man cocked one ear. "I hear a rider. Do you?"

"Anteros!" Adrestia's yell echoed toward him along with the pounding of her horse's hooves.

Adrestia shouldn't be out here in the forest, not when he'd left instructions for her to ready *The Cobra* for their trip to Algiers. He'd asked her to oversee the preparations and ensure all the supplies they'd require for the journey had been added to the hold.

Something important must have torn her away from that duty to bring her to him.

"I'm here!" he yelled back, then grasped Fedele's reins and mounted up, Giovani doing the same.

She flew around the bend and slowed as she caught sight of them. She brought her horse in alongside their horses and in her sandy-colored breeches and colorfully dyed cloak flapping over her mare's rump, pushed her hair away from her flushed cheeks. "Finally, I found you."

"What brings you out here to meet us, *Sorella*?" he asked her.

"It's Olivia." She reached across and seized his forearm. "I awoke this morning from a strange dream, as if I sensed she was in trouble, so I knocked on your bedchamber door and when she didn't answer, I barreled in. She wasn't there, Anteros, although I found a wad of cloth on the floor at the foot of your bed, one which reeked of belladonna."

His ears rang, his sister's words tumbling through his head.

She wasn't there—
Wad of cloth on the floor—
Belladonna.

"Anteros." Adrestia shook his arm. "She's been taken by Nazari. I'm certain of it."

"Has he set sail yet?"

"*Sì*, not long after midnight."

"Did anyone see anything suspicious? The castello is impenetrable. Olivia simply couldn't be gone."

"The guards saw nothing, and I awoke every servant in the house and had them check each and every room as well as the gardens and the stables. When she couldn't be found, I came straight to you."

"I—I shouldn't have left her alone. Nazari must have found a way in, although I've no idea how." His mind spun in a hundred different directions. "It's impossible. It's a fortress."

"What on earth does Nazari think he's doing?" Giovani's eyes narrowed to small slits. "Do you think he might be playing both sides?"

"I'm not sure, although he hates his father. He always has."

"What are your orders?" Adrestia fisted her reins, her back stiff and straight.

"We must make all haste, ride for home then set sail for Algiers." His horse pranced agitatedly under him. "And the moment we catch up to Nazari, I'm going to kill him."

He shoved his knees into his stallion's sides and with his head bent low over Fedele's neck, he galloped hard and fast, Adrestia and Giovani pounding behind him.

Olivia should have been safe on Paradiso. He'd failed her, which he'd promised himself would never happen.

The serpent deep within him hissed and rose.

Chapter 13

Everything spun as Olivia groggily opened her eyes. She blinked and tried to bring her surroundings into focus. She sat roped to a hard-backed chair on the creaky upper deck of a ship, bright sunshine bathing the blue waters of the sea, her wrists bound behind her, her fingers numb and arms pinned in place. Waves splashed over the side of the ship and sea-spray misted over her. She tipped her gaze up and caught the sails flapping overhead. Two topmen climbed up the ratlines and edged along the mizzen yard with daggers clasped between their teeth. Fierce winds pushed the ship to high speed.

"It's about time you awoke." Nazari's deep voice came from somewhere behind her.

"You've gone too far this time." Wriggling her fingers and toes, she got a little more sensation back. On port side, a thin line of land with orange sandhills rose. The Barbary Coast.

"This is your second fork in the road," he uttered.

"I can hardly spread my wings and fly if you've got my arms pinned down." She jiggled her chair, the legs scraping until she could crank her head around enough to eye Nazari seated at a desk in the covered room behind the helm, a map spread across the top of his desk with each corner of the map weighted with a dagger. She sent him her most venomous stare.

"You are taking your abduction far better than I expected." An arrogant smirk.

"How much longer until we reach the citadel?" Since she was to take the path that led to rescue and release, that meant she was on her way to where Hazim awaited her. Nothing else made sense. Huffing, she jostled her chair some more and uttered, "If you don't mind, would you please share the rest of Shira's plan since I'm clearly now an integral part of it."

"I've already shared all I can." Gracefully, he leaned back in his chair and idly crossed his arms behind his head, his white tunic open at his neck and linen sleeves rolled to his elbows.

"Anteros will kill you." She blew out a long breath, her hair a windswept mess flying in her face. "You do realize that don't you?"

"Only if he catches me." A chuckle and a wink.

She wanted to kick him, even jerked one foot forward but got nowhere as the rope binding her ankles cut into her skin. "You are the most detestable man I've ever had the misfortune to meet."

"Adrestia often states the same." He rocked his chair

onto the back two legs and held his position. "Please remember, I didn't have a choice in abducting you, not when Shira told me I must. May I release you from your bonds without being punched?"

"A lady doesn't punch a man." Yet if she could reach that iron bar propped in the corner, she would definitely swing it at him, even try to take off his head, no matter what Shira had commanded him to do.

"Wait there before you hurt yourself." He dropped back onto all four chair legs, stood and came around in front of his desk. Holding up his hands, he stepped closer. "I'm going to remove your bindings and allow you some freedom. Please, try to refrain from killing me or striking me. Do we have an agreement?"

"I'm not a savage as you are." Her fingers itched for that iron bar.

"True, but there is a fire in your eyes that currently reminds me of Adrestia's when I anger her." He came around behind her, knelt at her back and unknotted the ropes keeping her bound to the chair. Coiling the rope, he eased back in front and eyed her reddened wrists as she rubbed them. "How badly are you hurt?"

"Not as badly as you'll soon be." She pushed to her feet, stumbled into him with an "*oomph*," her stupid feet still bound.

"Sit down while I finish the job." He settled her back down.

"You are insufferable." She eased into the chair, stuck her feet out. "Hurry it along. I don't have all day to sit around when I must plan my own rescue and release."

"It's good to see your fighting spirit is intact, and that you listened to Shira's words I passed along to you." He removed the rope at her ankles and pins and needles stabbed through her toes as sensation returned.

"You are a tyrant." She heaved to her feet and swayed.

"Don't move too quickly." He caught her arms, held her steady.

"Let go of me." A wave crashed against the side of the ship, then the bow dropped down as they surged into deep water before rising back up and over the next high swell. He didn't release her, not until the ship had settled. When he finally stepped back, she tightened the belt of her lavender silk dressing robe and tottered to the rail. Clenching the wood smoothed by the many hands which had held onto it over the years, she asked, "Are you truly prepared to forsake your own flesh and blood?"

"I've been prepared since the day my father slaughtered my mother…in cold blood, I might add." He strode to the side table holding a jug. He poured apple cider into a mug and offered it to her.

She held the rail with one hand, tried to corral her whipping hair with the other. "A cup of tea would be lovely. Cream and sugar please."

"I don't have any tea." He plucked a leather strip from his pocket and held that out. "For your hair."

"You have absolutely no manners." Except beyond parched, she snatched the mug and gulped the cider down in a rather unladylike fashion, then she slammed the mug back into his chest and pinched the leather strip.

Leaning one hip against the railing, she carefully tied her hair back at her nape.

"I would like to explain my actions." He poured more cider into the mug, swigged the drink down himself. "I don't usually accost ladies. Tavern wenches, yes, but I usually do my best to keep them entertained in my bed before I return them."

"You are an abomination." Lifting the hem of her robe so she didn't trip on it, she gave him her back and leaned her elbows on the smooth wood. Taking a few deep breaths of the crisp sea air, she tried to expel the last dregs of the sedative. The shoreline wasn't all that far away, closer now than when she'd awoken. She could even make out patchy dry grass waving from within the sand dunes along the shoreline.

Carefully, she palmed her belly and sent a quick prayer skyward that her unborn child would continue to remain safe and unharmed. Clearing her throat, she asked over her shoulder, "Why would you force Anteros into this position? You'll have lost whatever trust you'd momentarily gained with him by this abduction."

"Unfortunately, my fate has always been to stand on the opposite side of the battle lines from him.'" Shrugging, he sat on one corner of his desktop. "I will always be Hazim's son, and he will always be Ferdinand's. Then there is the fact that my countrymen's way of survival is far different to his own. I am a corsair, the same as the men upon this ship. We pillage and plunder and steal. There is no other way for us, not if we wish to survive our enemies. The weakest die, while the strongest endure. That is simply how it is."

"You could change." She faced him, leaning back against the rail for support as she crossed her arms. "When we first met, you told me to call you Alessandro. May I call you that?"

He stared at her.

"May I?"

"Of course." He blinked with clear surprise. "Are we being friendly?"

"Alessandro, when we arrive at the citadel, I need you to take me to see Shira." He was currently holding her life in his hands and she needed to speak to Shira about it. "You may call me Olivia."

"If we are being friendly, then I need to warn you that any friendship with me will be complicated. I usually make a mess out of keeping friends." Gaze narrowed, he watched her alertly. "As Anteros would have told you."

"Everyone deserves a second chance, and I'm willing to give you one, provided you take me to see Shira."

"I agree to your request." He joined her at the side of the ship and rested his arms on the railing, his gaze going to the white-tipped waves. "Would you like to adjourn to one of the cabins below deck? I can offer you a change of clothes."

"Clothes suitable for a lady?"

"Exceedingly suitable. Come." He jogged down the short flight of steps to the foredeck and waited for her.

"I'm coming." She followed him below the deck and

down the companionway. At the last door, he stepped inside.

She entered the cabin and gasped.

The room was spacious, a large bed dominating one wall, a tall-standing wardrobe fixed to the other. A sitting area graced one corner, two armchairs covered in a royal blue brocade with an array of colorful pillows scattered on the floor between them. One could sit or lounge as they desired.

"You'll find what you need in the wardrobe." He stepped back.

She drifted closer to it, clutched a hand to her mouth as she spied the treasure within. "There are so many gowns. Dozens of them. Who are they all for?"

"The wenches."

"Oh, cease giving me that nonsense." She riffled through the gowns, the fabrics rich and luxurious. Elegant slippers and riding boots graced the elevated floor of the wardrobe, so fine and exquisitely made, and the shelves on the left held soft leather breeches and blouses and tunics similar to what Adrestia wore when captaining her ship. "I know who these clothes are for. We both know."

"Regardless of who I had them made for, they'll still grow musty and old since the woman in question will never wear them." He backed away toward the door. "Once you've changed, return to the helm. I'll be waiting for you, Olivia."

The door clicked shut behind him.

Well, it appeared Alessandro Nazari Hazim was a

man of many faces. He dreamed of a better life and whether he would ever have it or not, he still hoped for it. Which meant he might just be redeemable, no matter he'd abducted her.

She unknotted her belt, removed her dressing robe and nightgown, selected a clean chemise from the wardrobe and pulled it over her head. Quickly, she donned the first gown she plucked from the rail, the velvet soft with short sleeves and a square cut neckline edged in lace. The ruby skirts swished about her ankles, the high waist sitting perfectly.

She found some stockings, slid them on, then secured them with a garter before easing her feet into a pair of soft leather half-boots. From the shelves, she selected a hooded black robe and settled it over her shoulders before pulling the front ties together. She nabbed a veil and pocketed it before leaving the confines of the cabin and returning to the upper deck.

The sky had darkened, a vivid sunset orange-red now burning along the horizon.

She joined Nazari at the helm where he stood with his hands firm on the wheel. He tipped his head toward a tray of food sitting on his desk in the helm's quarters behind him.

"Help yourself," he offered.

"Thank you." Her belly rumbled as the exotic scent of the food swirled toward her. She selected a slice of the warm flatbread sprinkled with gooey cheese and bit into it. The thin curls of cheese on top danced with rich flavor on her tongue. She popped a stuffed date into her mouth next, then spied the tea pot and smiled. "Liar, liar, snip your tongue off and toss it in the fire."

He chuckled.

She laughed too. "During my childhood, my papa used to recite that to me whenever I spoke a mistruth." She poured herself a cup and added a splash of cream and a teaspoon of sugar. "Which was often enough that I recall it rather well." Saucer in hand, she returned to him as she sipped. "Tell me more about your relationship with Adrestia."

"We both have the same wild nature." The wind rose, swelled out his white tunic as the sun descended below the horizon, the last rays of the day glinting off his belted scimitar.

"You also have a history I'd like to know more about."

"We've ridden camels together across the desert," he admitted. "We've explored caves, hunted for food and often eaten the same meal over an open fire. There have been times over the years when we've gotten lost just looking into each other's eyes. Then there have been other times when we've battled and fought each other out at sea. Our relationship is the most complicated one I've ever had."

"How very interesting." She raised a brow, smiled. "I wed Anteros, so I understand complicated relationships rather well. I adore complicated."

"Unfortunately, so do I."

"I believe we might make good friends after all."

Chapter 14: Shira

In her small blue parlor, Shira Ria fell to her knees on a cushion and thumped her hands on the low parlor table, the weight of a powerful vision assailing her. Nazari had begun the battle to save both Anteros and Olivia by stealing Olivia away. Good gracious. Anteros would be furious when he learned of this abduction, but she prayed he would forgive her since she'd had no choice in the matter, Nazari too.

The images continued to swirl behind her closed eyelids. Images that moved from Olivia and Nazari on board the *Saif* to the dungeons below Hazim's palace.

Armed and dangerous, Hazim marched along the darkened lower passageways, his stride firm. She hurried to keep up with him, her senses assailed by the dank odor clinging to the gritty walls lit by torches braced in iron wall sconces.

Over the years, she'd walked along those passageways many-a-time, the wide network leading in all directions, although the only direction she ever took was directly between the cells and the slave pens. She'd always longed to free the children, each and every one of them, but those children came and went far too quickly, sold by Hazim.

Other than for Yakira.

He'd kept her these past six months as his plaything, her fierce spirit intriguing him at a time when very little did. Hazim wished to break the young woman, and he soon would, which meant time was running out. She needed to secure Yakira's freedom. Which was why Olivia's abduction had had to come into play.

She needed Anteros to fight not only for his and Olivia's survival, but also for all those Shira considered hers to care for. Yakira among them.

Within her vision, Hazim continued walking ahead.

She followed him, turned the corner and halted as he strode into one of the cells Barossa keep for those poor souls who provided him with amusement, foul and unfitting amusement.

Barossa stood shirtless in faded brown leather breeches before one of his chained prey, the slave woman dangling from a hook embedded in the ceiling, her thin arms straining and her coming death no doubt a slow and tortuous one. That was Barossa's way.

Shira hadn't seen this woman before though, so she must have been brought in recently.

Chains rattled from the woman's shackles, the heavy restraints swaying and the hem of her bloodied undertunic torn from ankle to thigh. The woman's face remained unmarred, but that would change at Barossa's hand. Hazim's youngest son had been conceived through black magic and tribal blood offerings. As such, Barossa had always held an evil streak that had grown even more evil with each year that passed.

With one arrogant brow raised, Hazim grasped Barossa's shoulder and eyed his son before releasing him and circling the slave. "A carrier bird arrived with a message. My watchmen have sighted Nazari's ship along the coastline. He will arrive not long after dark. Keep one of the cells free for *the cobra's* wife."

"Are you certain that Nazari has captured her?" Barossa stabbed the dangling slave in her side with his spear. The woman screamed and blood oozed forth in a splotch of red, her hair a matted mess with dirt and grit embedded in it.

"During my last reading with Shira," Hazim stated, "she assured me that the boy Paolo would deliver the missive I wrote, and that Nazari would ensure Anteros followed him after stealing his new bride away. I have every confidence that will happen."

"I don't trust the witch you seek readings from." Another stab. Another scream.

"That is because you haven't gained any control over Shira. You need to learn how to take advantage of her. Shira has weaknesses. Like the children in the slave pens. She cossets and cares for them. Those children are her greatest weakness, while yours is your temper." He pointed at his son. "Ensure a cell remains free as I requested and lay out the weapons I'll need to torture her with."

Hazim swung around and left.

She followed him to the next cell where he kept Yakira.

He pushed the iron-barred door open and halted where the meager light from a single candle illuminated the eighteen-year-old strapped to a wooden rack, her arms and legs bound to the cross, her head rising from a slump, her eyes dazed from her blood loss. She was running out of time.

"*Não me toques*. Leave me be." Yakira slumped her head forward again.

"You are an ungrateful wretch."

"Sir." A eunuch scurried into the cell, his head shaved and plain brown robes swaying. He apologized profusely before stating, "You asked to be informed when the sheikh arrived. His ship has dropped anchor in the bay. He and his son have entered the city and have been escorted by your guards to the rooms in the palace which you asked to have made ready for them."

"Ensure the sheikh's every comfort is seen to until I can join him."

"Of course." The eunuch dipped his head and rushed away.

Hazim seized Yakira's neck and watched as she struggled to breathe. Foam bubbled between her lips before he released his grip. Smirking, he waited as she wheezed and sucked in air. "We shall resume our session after I've visited with the sheikh. You should be thanking him for the fortunate timing of his arrival. He is here to bid for the best of my female slaves. Perhaps I shall offer him you."

Her vision slowly receded and Shira opened her eyes. Yes, she was definitely running out of time. For all of them.

Chapter 15

Only a few minutes ago, the sun had set in a blazing glory of orange and red along the horizon, the night sky now inky-black with stars studding it. Anteros kept an alert gaze on the waves ahead, every muscle in his body bunched rigid and tight, his palms firm on the wheel as he maintained his course across the Mediterranean toward Algiers. Adrestia laid a hand on his arm, his sister having not moved from his side since they'd set sail, and glad he was for her comforting presence. "I've amassed a large army of men, *Sorella,* built my trade and fleet of ships and placed myself in a position of power, but regardless of it all, I couldn't protect Olivia from within my own stronghold's walls."

"*Fratello,* the blame for this abduction lies entirely at Nazari's deceitful feet, not yours. We will find her, then we shall bring her home."

"We shall." He searched the darkened waters. "When we drop anchor, you will remain with the ship out of sight of the Bay of Algiers. Giovani and I will rendezvous with the traitor Nazari in his father's palace, just as Shira wished for in her plan."

"You intend on keeping to that plan?"

"What other choice do I have?" He squeezed his eyes shut, opened them again, a hundred different emotions roaring through him. "I trust Shira, even though I don't trust Nazari."

"The directive came from Shira, so you're right to keep with the plan."

"I'll do so, but Giovani and I shall take an elite team with us. We won't go in alone. You, meanwhile, will ensure our escape path remains intact. Are we agreed?"

"I won't let you down."

"*Grazie.*" He caught a lock of his sister's flying hair and tugged it just as Giovani bounded up the stairs to the helm in a white lawn shirt and black breeches, his saber swinging from his hip. "Have you assembled the team?" he asked his right-hand man.

"I have, and they're ready to depart the moment we drop anchor."

"*Buono.*" No one would keep him from retrieving his wife.

He would find her this night.

No other outcome would he allow.

Chapter 16

Seated at the bow, Olivia clutched the side of the skiff as Nazari rowed them both toward the beach, his ship moored out in the dark at the very edge of the Bay of Algiers.

Through the slits in her veiled headdress, she searched the eastern shoreline where torches glittered beyond the citadel's fortified walls. "Where exactly is Shira's home located?"

"Not far from the marketplace." As the hull scraped the sandy curve of the beach, Nazari set the oars inside then bounded over the side into the knee-deep waters. In a turban and djellaba, he gripped the bow and hauled it half up onto the shore, then holding out one hand, he uttered, "Come."

"Promise me again, that we're going to see Shira." She held back from accepting his offered hand.

"I promise." He crossed his hand over his heart, extended it to her again. "Now, come. Life can't be lived without a little bit of danger. It's time for that danger to begin."

"Since leaving England and becoming Anteros's wife, I've learned that fact very well." She placed her hand in Nazari's outstretched hand and allowed him to aid her from the skiff onto the sand.

Together, they walked up the beach toward the outer stone wall which surrounded the citadel and with her heartbeat racing, she passed several cannons mounted on slabs of stone.

"We'll be entering through one of the postern gates. Do not look at the sentry guards. Do not speak a word. Remain absolutely quiet." He caught her elbow and guided her around the fortified stone wall until they reached a cobbled path that led up a sandy rise.

When they reached the end of that path, they hit the sand and she pushed onward, the sand slithering downhill with each step she took uphill. Once they reached the top, Nazari swept an arm around her shoulders and guided her toward an iron door set in the wall. At Nazari's call, a guard swung the gate open and waited for them to enter. They stepped inside and the guard closed the iron gate with a clank.

"We must keep moving. This way." Through the shadows within the city, he guided her.

With an eerie chill settling into her bones, she hurried with him through the streets to the main square of the marketplace, stalls of brightly colored tents and awnings now closed for the night, the faint aroma of spice still lingering in the air. Running her tongue over her teeth, she caught the dusty grit of sand from the desert which had somehow made its way into her mouth.

Following Nazari, she trekked down a side street where pastel-painted houses stood wall to wall. Rope swayed high over her head, strung between the balconies with washing pinned to it, the night breeze flapping the washing about. "Is this the street where Shira lives?"

He didn't answer her question, but instead said, "This is where we'll borrow a horse which will allow us to travel to her home faster."

He hoisted her onto the back of a horse secured to a wooden post, released the reins and swung up behind her. Arms braced either side of her, he thrust his knees into the horse's flanks and urged the horse into a gallop.

He rode hard through the streets, negotiating with skilled ease the tight twists and turns of the road leading uphill. As they crested the hill, he slowed and jerked to a halt before the gates of a sprawling, heavily patrolled fortress. Curved arches supported by pillars graced the front of the two story palace, the crowned roof holding raised domes and the dey's flag flying from the uppermost point of his fortress.

Her heart sank into her gut.

He hadn't taken her to Shira as she'd requested.

"I placed my trust in you, Alessandro." She glared at him. "You clearly had no intention of honoring your promise to take me to Shira."

"I can't deliver you to Shira, not when she told me I couldn't. She said you would ask, that I was to allow you to believe I would, but in all truth, there are more lives at risk this day than just yours." He searched her gaze. "Please, you must listen to me. To save your life, I must first place it in jeopardy. Those are Shira's words. Hold tight to them. Trust in them. Even when I hand you over to my father."

"Please, don't hand me over to Hazim."

"I must. It's time for you to take the path that leads to rescue and release. Remember, that is the path where Shira watches over us all, always and forever." He turned to the guard at the gatehouse, lifted his voice and called out, "Awaken Dey Hazim. I bring Her Royal Highness, the Duchess of Paradiso to him."

The gates cranked open.

Chapter 17

On the deck of his ship, Anteros donned a black headdress and swung an equally dark cloak over his shoulders, the faint scent of orange blossoms curling around him. He dragged the collar to his nose and drew in more of Olivia's lingering scent. He hadn't expected it to still be on this cloak. During his last sea voyage—a short trip to Sicily a few weeks prior—he'd stepped in behind her as she'd been standing at the bow, the hour of night upon them. He'd wrapped this very cloak around her shoulders, one he'd taken from his own wardrobe and when she'd turned with a sweetly sensual smile and looked into his eyes, he'd gently fastened the ties, leaned in and nuzzled her cheek.

His heart clenched hard at that memory.

A memory that beat with a heavy and mangled

throb in his chest.

Olivia had changed him, made him more vulnerable, but she'd also changed him for the better, and she belonged to him, was his to keep safe.

Which meant there wasn't a chance he'd allow Nazari to remain alive after what he'd done in taking his very heart from him. Whether it was part of Shira's plan or not, he couldn't permit his enemy—any of his enemies—to believe they could do the same and expect to live. Yes, there was far more at stake here than he'd ever imagined. Nazari had stirred the cobra within him, brought the hissing serpent swiftly to the surface. No one placed Olivia's life, or that of his unborn child's, in danger.

He marched toward the bow, gripped the railing and squeezed his eyes tightly shut in an attempt to rein in his fierce emotions. He couldn't lead his team of men if he didn't have a clear head. Footsteps clipped across the deck and he opened his eyes as Giovani joined him.

"The men are ready to depart." Giovani gave him a questioning look. "Are you ready to leave?"

"I am." He motioned to his men awaiting him, gave them the signal to lower the skiff over the side of the ship into the waves. As they followed his command, he plucked a tin from his pocket and vigorously rubbed black soot over his face to hide his features. He handed Giovani the tin and he scrubbed soot over his face too before passing the tin to each of the remaining four men he'd handpicked for this mission. A small team, but an elite team. Each man had the skills he needed if he wished to sneak into the palace without being seen.

He climbed down the roped netting, dropped into the skiff bobbing on the night-shrouded water and once they were on board, they rowed to the shoreline a mile distant from the citadel.

With satchels strapped to their backs, they trekked across the rocky and dry coastal terrain to the very edge of the fortified walls of the Kasbah of Algiers.

Within twenty feet of a secret entrance he'd used in the past, the covert route one that very few knew about, he lowered to a crouch in the sand and raised a hand for his men to do the same. Long minutes ticked by as he waited to ensure no guards roamed the area.

Once assured all remained clear, he stole inside the wall through the small hidden gap.

With his back shoved against the inner stonework, he waited.

Still no movement, no guards about. Perfect.

After releasing a soft whistle, he waited for his men and they appeared beside him, one after the other along the wall. Thank heavens for the waning moon, that it barely lit the night sky.

He scanned his surroundings, as did his men. During the day, this city burst with life and vibrancy, the people of Algiers swarming about the busy marketplace. Within the souk, buyers haggled with the stall vendors, the air filled with the scents of mint tea, strong coffee, and a multitude of oriental spices, although once the dark of the night descended, everything changed.

Everything became darker, deadlier. As it did now.

Everyone knew to seek sanctuary in their homes, although there would be no sanctuary for him this night. It was time to go.

"Let's separate into two teams," he instructed Giovani, "as we discussed before leaving the ship. We've less of a chance of getting caught if we do."

"Agreed. We'll meet you at the rendezvous point." Giovani motioned to two of his men, then disappeared into the dark with them.

"We'll take the southern route." He gave the command and set out, his men close on his heels.

He and Giovani would meet up at the entrance to the tunnel. A tunnel which ran below Algiers toward the palace that sat high on the hill overlooking the ocean, the tunnel one that his grandfather had shown him during his first visit to Algiers as a lad. He'd been so young, but he'd never forget the excitement and danger as he'd dropped into the tunnel and explored the darkest recesses of Algiers.

Certainly, the element of surprise would be needed this night, and that tunnel would provide it.

Through the tight streets, he made his way, slowing his pace here and there, while in other places moving briskly, his men following suit. The higher uphill they trekked, the more uneven the cobbles got under his feet.

Somewhere up ahead, the rumbling growl of a camel echoed toward him and he halted as riders entered the street. With no time to spare, he and his men ducked into a darkened alleyway, squeezing into the small space between two buildings. The riders passed by in uniform—the dey's personal guard. He waited, a bird squawking as it landed awkwardly on the swaying branch of a nearby fig tree.

Once all was quiet again, he gave the order to continue onward.

Long minutes passed as they ducked and dived between houses until they finally reached the rendezvous point.

Giovani appeared out of the dark, having arrived at the same time as them. "You had no issue?" Anteros asked his man.

"We came across two patrols but kept out of their sight. What about you, Anteros?"

"One patrol, although I expected far more. Are you ready to continue?"

"*Sì*, after you." Giovani gestured to the channel running below the curved bridge up ahead, a channel currently devoid of any water, although when the rains came, that channel flowed with rainwater which collected in the reservoir a little farther downhill.

"Follow me." Carefully, Anteros moved out,

skidded down the slope, the sandy ground loose underfoot until he hit a half-hidden grate. On his knees, he dug the orange grains free from around the edge of the iron. With a heave, he lifted the grate that creaked open before he gently lowered it beside the hole.

He pulled a rope from his satchel, handed it to Giovani who knotted one end around his waist and sat on the embankment. Giovani braced his feet in place, and Anteros nabbed the other end of the rope, swung down into the cavernous dark and landed on the ground inside the tunnel. He lifted his gaze and eyed the hole he'd dropped through. "Send everyone down."

Each of his men dropped into the tunnel beside him, then Giovani dangled one-handed from the rim, managed to pull the grate back into place after himself, and released his grip on the metal bars. His man landed with his knees bent.

"Light the torches we brought, Marco." Anteros waited as Marco lit them and handed them out. "*Grazie*." He gripped Marco's shoulder, cast his gaze between each of his men. "We've sailed together for years, undertaken dangerous missions, but tonight's mission is the most important we'll ever embark on. We must find my wife and bring her home. I'll take the lead."

He set out, his men falling in behind him, the stone base of the tunnel uneven.

They climbed uphill for at least half a mile before

they reached a divide in the tunnel.

He took the left passageway which led directly to the palace.

"We'll be there soon," he breathed in promise to his wife, although still not soon enough for his liking.

Chapter 18

Crowded walls hemmed Olivia in as she entered the restricted area of the Dey of Algiers's palace.

"Do exactly as I say," Nazari warned her in a harsh whisper as he nudged her along. "Keep your gaze fixed on the floor, and do not speak to anyone unless I say you may."

"Everyone already knows who I am, Alessandro. You announced the news at the main gate." She'd wanted to rake her nails down his face when he'd done that. "I believe you need to better explain this plan of Shira's. At what point does the rescue and release occur?"

"Shh, quiet." Grasping her arm, he marched her between two colossal pillars.

Bristling, she clamped her lips together as she entered a massive open room with walls covered in thin, shimmery gold curtains. Overhead, the ceiling arched high, while at her feet, the white floor tiles were flecked with gold. At the head of the room sat a raised dais furnished with plush divans and multicolored cushions with more sheer silk drapes rippling in an array of exotic colors behind the high platform.

"My father comes." That was all the warning he gave her before a tall, dark-haired man entered through a gap in the silk drapes.

A white cloak with fancy gold embroidery flowed loosely over Hazim's white tunic and baggy, long trousers caught at his ankles. At his right hip, a curved blade embedded with yellow and red precious stones, gleamed. With a scowl on his face, one that appeared set in perpetual stone, the Dey of Algiers strode toward her.

She dropped her gaze to the floor and patted her headdress to ensure her veil remained in place. She would follow Nazari's instructions. This was his father, and no one knew Hazim better than his own son.

Hazim circled her, his hot breath fanning the back of her neck through the layers of her clothing, his shadow passing across the floor until he once more stood in front of her. In a harsh, low growl he ordered, "Look at me."

She lifted her chin only enough to glance at Nazari to seek his approval.

"Father." Nazari stepped closer to her. "The duchess is aware she may not speak to anyone unless I say she may."

"Is that so, my son?" Hazim spat. The Dey of Algiers withdrew a lethal scimitar holstered to his back, the eerie slide of steel on steel freezing Olivia in place.

He slid his curved blade snugly around her nape in a metallic embrace of death.

Death. Death. Death.

His evil gaze promised it.

Ice trickled through her blood.

He was going to end her life right now, slice her head right from her shoulders, the curved blade ensuring a clean cut. Her heart thudded like thunder in her own ears.

Nazari grasped Hazim's shoulder. "Think carefully before you use that blade on *the cobra's wife*."

"I have no intention of killing her, not when I have a cell prepared for her." Hazim laughed, his scimitar pricking her skin. "I've dreamed of the torture I intend on inflicting on her. Granting her a quick death isn't something I'm prepared to offer her."

Her knees trembled, Nazari's earlier words echoing through her head. *To save your life, I must first place it in jeopardy.* Well, her life was certainly in jeopardy, and she truly couldn't wait for the whole saving part to begin. Why on earth would Shira have constructed such a plan?

Another prick from Hazim's blade.

Blood dripped warm and wet down her neck.

Chapter 19

Anteros held his position in the tunnel. Above his head, a wide grate allowed light to penetrate through. He and his grandfather had stood in this very spot over thirteen years ago. The two of them had grabbed this grate, heaved it up and hoisted themselves to the next level, then they'd walked along the dungeon passageway holding cells on each side. Tonight, he'd revisit those dungeons once more.

He gave Giovani a silent nod to boost him up. His man cupped his palms, and he placed his foot in them and got leveraged higher. High enough to push the grate quietly aside. Gripping the wide rim the grate had sat in, he pulled himself even higher and climbed through the opening.

Swiftly, he moved into a crouch on the gritty floor, his palm sliding around the hilt of his belted saber. Up ahead, a candle glowed from an iron wall sconce, the air swirling with the coppery scent of blood.

Giovani hoisted himself up next and stepped in beside him, his other men swiftly following suit, each of them spreading out along the passageway. He gave the silent signal that he intended on moving forward, directly toward the bend up ahead.

Slow movements. He kept his step light. Guards patrolled these lower recesses.

With one finger, he stepped past the barred doorway of a cell and caught movement within. A woman was bound to a torture rack, her arms and legs spread wide and blood trickling down her sides and dripping onto the floorboards. She had long, dark hair, her bottom covered in welts, her head slumped forward. Whatever she'd been wearing had been reduced to rags that swayed in tatters from her shoulders.

In his ear, Giovani whispered, "She fits the description Paolo gave us of Yakira before we set sail."

"If it's Yakira, then she's coming with us." Anteros released the unlocked catch and opened the door. He slipped into the cell, raised one-finger to his lips. "I don't mean you any harm. *Nenhum mal.* Are you Yakira?" he asked in her native Portuguese.

She lifted her chin, exhaustion lining her face, although a quiet strength sparked in her eyes. She was a fighter. She wanted to live, and he intended on making sure that happened.

"Are you Yakira?" he asked again.

"*Eu sou*. I am." She strained against her bindings. "Who are you?"

"I'm *the cobra*. Paolo sent me."

"You've seen Paolo?" She rattled her chains. "Please, is he well?"

"He's faring far better than you."

"Free me. I beg it of you."

"As it happens, I'm not leaving without you. Tito, release her. Marco, hand her your cloak." His men moved forward and while Tito released her bonds, Marco swung his cloak from his shoulders and wrapped her in it. She limped clear of the rack. Both men propped the young woman up with an arm around her waist, kept her steady. "Right, we have very little time to waste. We move out with all speed," he instructed his men.

With his headdress covering his face, he slipped through the door and moved with stealth down the stony corridor. Once he reached the uneven stairs, he snuck up them and entered another walkway and there, standing in the shadows up ahead, a heavily armed guardsman stood on duty.

Without a noise, he snuck in behind the guard, caught the man in a choke hold, one arm wrapped around his neck and the other over the guard's mouth to ensure he didn't yell out a warning. The guard clawed at his hands and tried to wrench them free, but he simply tightened his hold until the guard succumbed to the pressure on his windpipe and slumped.

After a nod at Giovani, he silently lowered the man to the floor and rolled him into the shadows near the corner where the candlelight didn't reach. Giovani stayed with him, tight on his tail. Marco remained at the rear aiding Yakira whose cheeks were now flushed. A good sign, as was the eagerness in her eyes to escape this prison. His other three men moved to the other side of the darkened passageway.

"I expected to see more guards than we have," Giovani murmured in his ear.

"As have I." Although he wouldn't take their current good fortune for granted. "To the receiving hall we go. We're so close."

Brandishing his saber, he picked up his pace, although that good fortune came to a swift halt as he rounded the next bend. Two uniformed guards strode toward him, the door to the receiving hall halfway between them. So close. No time to stop. He bounded into the receiving hall, his men hard on his tail, and the guards' footsteps thundering as they made chase.

He shoved shimmery silk curtains out of the way and there, near the dais, three people stood under the high-arched ceiling. One was Nazari, the second Hazim, and the third a robed woman wearing a dark veil that hid her face. Hazim stood with his curved scimitar sitting snugly around the woman's neck, a woman Anteros knew well. Olivia—the other half of his heart.

He hauled off his headdress, swiped at the soot on his face, and tossed the linen aside. Hazim stood in a flowing white tunic and loose trousers gathered at his ankles, a white cloak with gold embroidery swaying from his shoulders. He marched toward the man "Hazim, I received an invitation and have now arrived."

Hazim lowered his scimitar and smirked before stalking toward him. "By way of invitation, you must mean the capture of your wife. What fortunate timing you have. Your bride will be able to witness your death before I toss her into the dungeons and torture her. I'm looking forward to hearing her screams as I whip her."

"Father." Nazari uttered his father's name in warning, tucked Olivia in behind him, and eyed Anteros. "Welcome to Algiers. Good of you to arrive, my old friend."

"You abducted my wife." He jabbed a finger at Nazari. "I'm going to kill you, right after I've killed your father." A commotion sounded behind him. The two guards giving chase had arrived. They swept into the room and Giovani scooped a marble vase from a table and slung it at the first guard. It hit the uniformed man square in the forehead and he groaned, his eyes rolling until the whites showed. The guard fell to his knees then hit the floor with his face. Tito whipped in behind the second guard and holding his saber high, slammed the hilt down on his head. The man slumped on top of his comrade. Anteros faced Hazim once again and arched a brow. "Those two guards might live, but you won't be as fortunate."

"I have dozens of guards, and they'll be arriving at any moment."

"Leave your guards out of this fight. It has always been between you and me, Hazim."

"Come. Allow me to send you to your grave." Hazim heaved his scimitar and Anteros bounded in, their blades clashing dead center, steel ringing loud against steel. More of Hazim's guards swarmed in and Anteros's men swung their sabers. Hazim sliced his blade toward Anteros's middle and would have connected if he hadn't jerked back. "This is my palace," Hazim bit out as he advanced. "You'll soon be outnumbered, *the cobra* dead at my hand."

At his back, Anteros's men continued to battle hard and fast, their blades flying. Giovani took a nasty nick to his chin before bellowing and slaying his adversary with one deadly slice across his chest. Blood spurted.

"Dying isn't on my agenda, although ensuring your death is." Anteros rebounded into his battle with Hazim. Their blades connected, over and over, then Hazim raised his sword arm and Anteros took the opening, dived in and speared his saber deep into Hazim's gut. He slashed and opened Hazim's gut, and

his enemy's innards spilled forth onto the tiled floor in a gory mess. Hazim hit the ground with a sickening thud, his jowls flapping but no noise leaving his lips.

Olivia trembled from behind Nazari.

Anteros left Hazim's body behind and moved swiftly toward her, except Nazari was still in his way. He pressed the tip of his blade against Nazari's throat. "Do you have any last words, traitor?"

"Shira recommended I not say a word at this point in her plan." Nazari raised his weaponless hands. "Except I would be remiss if I didn't say thank you for what you've just done. My father has finally paid for his sins, his execution absolute at your hand." Nazari gestured behind Anteros, Giovani and his men now wiping their blades and sheathing them, the guardsmen's bodies piled high, a river of red running across the floor. "You've now eliminated my father's personal guard, men who were loyal only to him, and for that I'm doubly grateful."

"Anteros." Olivia grasped Nazari's arm from behind. "Shira sent Nazari to abduct me. She told him that to save my life, he had to first place it in jeopardy. Shira's plan of attack always included my abduction. We just weren't made aware of that until it had already occurred."

"Your wife is right." Nazari stepped aside, allowed Olivia to pass and she ran into his arms. He held her tight as Nazari continued, "My part in Shira's plan is now complete, but yours still continues. You must go to Shira. She awaits you out at sea."

"Out at sea? What riddles are you speaking now, Nazari?"

"I speak the truth. Shira told me that she'd keep us at the forefront of her visions, that after you'd arrived at Algiers, she would meet Adrestia where you dropped anchor. Trust me, Shira will be on board your ship. You must leave now." Nazari motioned to the door. "There are other guards who will have been alerted by the commotion. Head north through the palace. There's an exit point from the kitchens that leads into the rear gardens."

"What about you?" Holding Olivia close, he sheathed his blade.

"Algiers needs a commander who cares about the people of Algiers."

"You're going to take on that role?"

"I will do my very best." Nazari offered Olivia a deep bow. "Travel safely, Olivia."

"You deserved a second chance, and I gave it. Stay alive, Alessandro." She pulled her veil free and dropped it. "And in the future, may you and I weather better storms than what has come to pass this day."

"I did warn you that any friendship with me would be complicated."

"Yes, that you did." Smiling, she turned to Anteros and looked deep into his eyes. "I've missed you, *Amati*. Take me home."

"You're never leaving me again. Home we go."

He kissed the tip of her nose and rushed her out of the receiving hall.

He'd never been more eager to leave Algiers behind, except safety was still some distance away.

They needed to take all care, and all speed.

Chapter 20

Panting, Olivia hurried through the passageways of the palace with Anteros and Giovani and four of her husband's men as well as a young woman wearing a dark cloak. She appeared battered and bruised and if Olivia wasn't mistaken, held a familial likeness to Paolo. "Please, Anteros. Tell me that's Yakira."

"It's Yakira. We found her in the dungeons. This way." He kept them moving with all speed even as footsteps approached from up ahead. Before they ran into the guards, Anteros veered to the right and they tore down a secondary passageway and rounded a bend, the heavy footsteps thankfully tapering away.

"How did you get inside the palace?" She had a thousand questions.

"By way of the dungeons through the underground tunnels, although that way will be compromised due to the trail of guards we left in our wake. The only way out of here is as Nazari said, by heading north to the kitchens. There's an exit point there and it leads through the rear gardens toward the cliffs." Anteros kept urging her along.

"Not far now," Giovani added as he slipped ahead of them.

"How is it you both know the lay of this palace so well?" She puffed, one hand on her side as she caught a cramp.

"A man always knows his enemy's lair."

A guard suddenly stepped into their path and Giovani swung, his fisted blow connecting with the guard's jaw which sent the man hurtling into the wall. His nose cracked and blood spurted as he slithered to the floor and fell with a crash. Giovani shoved the man out of the way and Anteros pulled her past the fallen guard and hurried them along.

Up ahead, the heavenly aroma of fresh bread wafted toward them and then they burst through a door into the kitchens where two aproned servants stirred stew in pots.

Holding one finger to his lips, Anteros moved toward them, "Don't be alarmed. My men and I mean you no harm. We simply require safe passage through these kitchens to the rear gardens."

Chapter 21

"Anteros?" One of the women uttered Anteros's name as she stepped up to him, wisps of gray hair escaping her scarf. She grasped his hands and smiled. "Do you remember me? We've eaten together at Shira's home. I'm her cousin."

"Aisha?" He frowned as he squeezed Aisha's hands. "Of course I remember you. You make the best *harira* I've ever tasted."

"Shira sent me, told me to await your arrival here." She beamed as she cast her gaze to Giovani. "*Marhaba*, Giovani. Where Prince Anteros treads, so too do you."

"You look as ravishing as always, Aisha." Giovani hauled her into a hug, kissed both her cheeks then set her back on her feet. "You're truly here at Shira's bidding?"

"She gave me the task of guiding you and your men out of the palace. My cousin awaits you out at sea." She handed her wooden spoon to the kitchen maid and told her not to speak a word of what she'd seen or heard, then beckoned them to follow her as she hurried across the kitchens to the far door. "Come, everyone. This way."

Anteros clutched Olivia's hand and urged her along after him. "It appears, *Amore*, that Shira has informed everyone other than you and me about her plan of attack." He would deal with Shira when he next saw her.

"Shira told me it had to be that way," Aisha stated as she pushed the door open. "No one knows the future like a seer. Trusting her is essential." She lifted a lit torch from the iron holder on the wall and disappeared down a passageway.

"Well, you have a point there," he admitted. Motioning for Giovani to bring the others, he steered Olivia after Aisha.

When they reached the end of the short corridor, Aisha motioned to a lock on the door. "Once we're outside, we need to follow the outer wall toward the cliffs. Adrestia and Shira will be awaiting us at the cove."

"Step back." He edged past Aisha, pulled his pistol and shot the lock. It blasted into pieces, the door swinging open. After rushing Olivia outside, he caught her up his arms and yelled for the others to follow.

He sprinted through the night-shrouded dark, the humid heat of the desert flowing thick and heavy all around, freedom so close at hand. Over rockery and bushes, he bounded, the rear courtyard filled with terraced gardens edged by the mountainous cliffside which protected the palace from the seaward side.

"We're almost at the edge." Olivia clutched ahold of his neck, her warm breath caressing his cheek and her long golden locks blowing back in the wind, her hood torn away. "I can run just as well as the others, *Amati*. Put me down."

"Not yet." The cliffs appeared out of the dark and he skidded to a stop, the tips of his boots teetering on the edge. Stones crumbled free and pinged down the cliff face before getting swallowed by the watery blackness far below. He pushed back a step and lowered Olivia to her feet as Aisha joined them. "How do we get down there, Aisha, without jumping that is."

"There's a tunnel that leads to the beach." Aisha hunkered down next to a ring of large boulders and pulled at shrubbery. "The entrance is right here next to these rocks."

"Let me help you." Giovani dropped to his knees and helped haul the shrubbery away until they'd uncovered the hidden entrance to the tunnel.

"I'll go first." Anteros gripped the edge of the entrance and dropped into the darkness below. "Pass me your torch," he called up to Aisha. She handed it down, and he waved it about to light the tunnel. All appeared clear, the tunnel falling away steeply where it ran downhill toward the cove. He jammed the torch into a crevice in the gritty wall and lifted his hands. "You're next, Olivia."

"I'm coming." She got down onto her bottom, her feet dangling over the rim, then she shuffled forward and he caught her around the waist and eased her onto her feet beside him. Next came Aisha, then Yakira. The three ladies huddled together as Giovani and the rest of his men dropped down into the tunnel beside him.

"Giovani, take the lead." He plucked the torch free and taking the rear with Olivia, followed his men as they trekked downhill. In some places he had to push past clinging bushes growing into the gritty sides of the tunnel, and in others he had to bend half over so he didn't hit his head where the tunnel got lower and thinned.

"Are you all right?" Olivia asked as she looked at him, the torchlight flickering across her beautiful face.

"I'm fine now that I have you back. Watch your step. This pathway is incredibly steep."

"What an adventure this has been, hmm?" A glow suffused her cheeks.

"An adventure we haven't yet gotten clear of." A gust of wind suddenly whistled up and he curled one arm around her waist and held her close as she swayed. Another gust of wind blew but this time brought with it the salty scent of the sea. "I can hear the ocean."

"So can I," Olivia whispered.

"We're here!" Giovani shouted from up ahead, the others having disappeared.

"Let's go." Holding her hand, he walked out of the tunnel and joined his right-hand man on the beach where the waves rolled in. Two skiffs sat beached farther along the curve of the cove, Shira and a handful of his crew standing before one skiff, and Adrestia the other.

"*Masaa el kheer!*" Shira waved. "Do hurry along, everyone. We don't have all night."

"Shira, there you are." He marched toward her, his frustration slowly melting away with each step he took. Shira had kept Olivia safe during her abduction, had successfully allowed him to retrieve his wife. He'd also been able to find and free Yakira, and would soon reunite the young woman with her brother. Lastly, he'd been given the opportunity to finally fell his greatest enemy. Hazim was gone, and now Algiers would be ruled a new commander—Nazari. He didn't doubt that Nazari would do far more good for the people of Algiers than Hazim ever had. Grinning, he scooped Shira close and squeezed her. "*Habeebi.* Thank you for looking after us all."

"I always will, and always shall, my beloved boy."

"*Fratello.*" Adrestia jumped into his arms and he laughed as he twirled her around.

His men cheered from the deck of his ship bobbing in the bay.

"It's time to go home." Olivia entwined her hand with his, reached onto her toes and kissed him.

"*Sì*, beyond time," he whispered against her lips, his very heart once more returned to him.

Chapter 22

With Anteros's hands on her waist, Olivia got boosted from the second of the two skiffs onto the ship and once aboard, she got smothered in Adrestia and Shira's wonderfully warm embrace again. Blinking back a tearful smile, she looked into Shira's eyes. "You are a master planner."

"I'm sorry I couldn't share it all with you, but my plan wouldn't have come to full fruition if I had." Cupping one wrinkled hand to her cheek, Shira smiled. "My child, you and Anteros, as well as Nazari and Yakira and Paolo have all been rescued during the undertaking of this plan, as well as the other children in the slave pens too. Nazari will set them free before this night is done."

"Then you are forgiven for all of the secrecy."

"It was such an incredible plan." Adrestia turned

from Shira and glanced toward the palace sitting high on the hill beyond the cliffs, the moon shimmering over the dark cliff face and lighting the craggy edges with silver. "Will Nazari be all right though, Shira?"

"Nazari no longer has to abide by Hazim's will, but he will still have to navigate the treacherous waters of Algiers. Hazim has governed for a long time and as I've learned, only the strongest survive, which means Nazari will need to keep a close eye on all of those around him, particularly Barossa. His half-brother, unfortunately, is more evil than his father."

"I've heard it said Barossa was born the spawn of black magic." Concern slashed Adrestia's brow as she eyed Shira. "Is that true?"

"Sadly, yes." Shira looked into Adrestia's eyes. "My sweet girl, there is something I need you to do. During the dark days to come, you must be Nazari's guiding light, the one who leads him toward the truth and not the edge of oblivion."

"That sounds like an impossible task."

"It will be a task that will shape and define you. That is for certain." Shira squeezed Adrestia tight and reached a hand to Yakira. She caught both of the young woman's hands in hers and rubbed them together. "You and I must speak, Yakira. How do you feel?"

"As if I've been given a second *oportunidade* at life." A tear escaped Yakira's eyes as she pulled Shira into a hug, her cloak secured tightly about her. "I am most grateful for my rescue. Will I see Paolo soon?"

"On the morrow, at first light," Shira promised as she extended a hand to Aisha and pulled her in close to her and Yakira. "Now, my cousin and I will remain at your side in the coming days. You and Paolo will need us, and we will not forsake you."

"That is true." Aisha gently brushed her fingers over the mottled bruise on Yakira's cheek. "Will you allow Shira and I to take care of you and your brother?"

"I will be most grateful for any care that both of you offer." Tears streamed down Yakira's cheeks.

"You have been through a terrible ordeal." Shira wiped Yakira's tears away. "Adrestia has already given us a cabin for the night. There are three bunks and I requested meals and clean clothes. We shall eat together. Come." Shira and Aisha led Yakira below deck.

"I pray Yakira will be able to heal from her time as Hazim's prisoner." Olivia kept her words quiet, ensuring they traveled no farther than Adrestia. The elite team of men who'd returned with Anteros had congregated around him and Giovani near the bow, Anteros offering the men his greatest thanks.

"While Shira and I were waiting for you on the beach, she told me that she and Aisha had already agreed that they will return with us, as well as remain at the castello to aid in Yakira and Paolo's recovery. Those two children should never have lost their parents so young in life or been forced to ensure the hardships they did at Hazim's hands."

"My papa passed away when I was seventeen, so I understand a little of their loss." She would be there for them too.

"*Sorella*," Anteros called to his sister with a wave then strode away from his men and took ahold of his sister's shoulders. He leaned in, kissed both her cheeks before rattling off a stream of Italian, his gratitude clear to hear in his affectionate tone. "Will you take us home?"

"I surely will." Adrestia left them, bounded up to the helm and took the wheel. Giovani joined her as she shouted orders to the crew.

"Come, *mio angelo*, you need your rest. *Immediatamente*." Anteros steered her toward the stairs, hurried her down the companionway and into his captain's quarters. He kicked the door shut behind him, gathered her in his arms and captured her mouth with his. He plundered between her lips, devouring her until she arched her body into his.

Desire rushed through her. "The bed is behind you." She nudged his chest and pushed him backward. "Two more steps."

"I know exactly where our bed is." He twirled her about, settled her on the end of the sapphire quilted cover and on one knee before her, plucked off her leather-soled half boots and tossed them aside. "Are you unharmed, *Amore*?"

"I may have been abducted, but at no time during that abduction did Nazari ever allow any true harm to come to me." With his cheeks cupped in her hands, she stroked her fingers back and forth along his stubbly jaw and released a happy sigh. "You found me, and now we're together again."

"Always and forever," he murmured.

The ship moved, the momentum toppling her back onto the mattress.

She giggled as he stood and loomed over her, the handle of his pistol glinting from his waistband. "You are still armed and dangerous, *Amati*."

"That will always be the case." He removed his weapons before settling himself comfortably beside her. Gently, he pulled her into his arms and held her tight. "How is our *bambino*?"

"Unharmed as well." She pushed her fingers into his dark hair, his locks so silky and soft. "Tell me this is real, that we're back together again."

"This is real, and we're most certainly back together again." He kissed her, his mouth moving over hers with a gentle reverence that spoke of his love for her, one hand protectively curling over her belly where their child lay. "I have never known such a heart-wrenching love as this. No more separation."

"Agreed. No more separation." A yawn escaped her.

"Why don't you rest for a while?"

"It has been a long day." She closed her eyes and

curled up against his warmth. "I do feel sleepy."

"Then sleep. We'll awaken together in the morn."

"Yes, we certainly will." She wanted nothing more than that simple pleasure, to awaken with him in the morning, and each and every morning to come. With the smooth rocking of the ship, she fell blissfully toward sleep with her prince holding her close.

In the morn, a new day would dawn…

A day that would lead to yet another adventure…

She didn't doubt it, not when their destiny guaranteed it.

She'd married a pirate prince.

Her pirate prince.

144

Sweet Regency Tales

The Duke Who Stole My Heart, Book 1
The Earl I Adore, Book 2
To Love During War, Book 3
My Secret and the Earl, Book 4
The Prince Who Captured Me, Book 5
Beware of the Pirate Prince, Book 6
My Infamous Corsair, Book 7 (Coming late 2020)

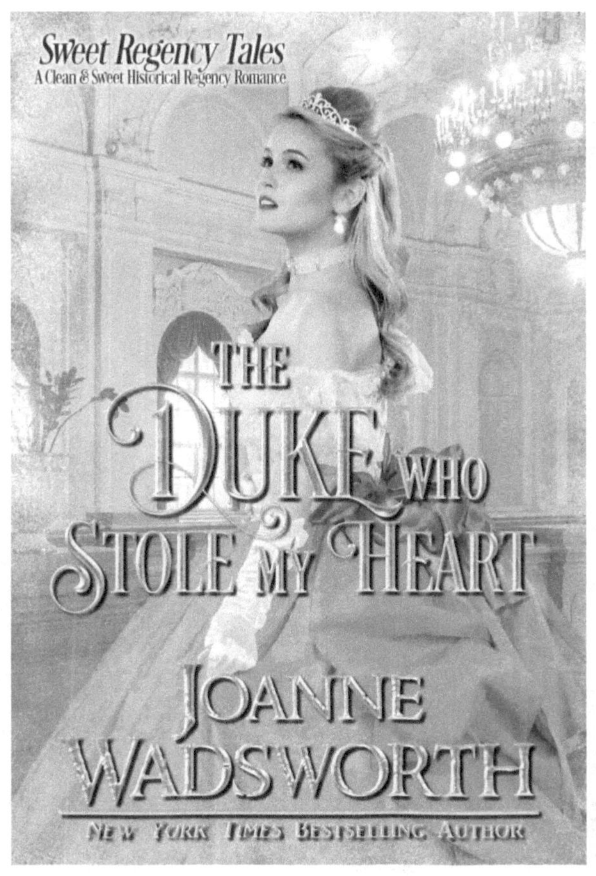

Want to Try a Time Travel Series?

Highlander's Desire, Book 1

Scottish Historical Time Travel Romance

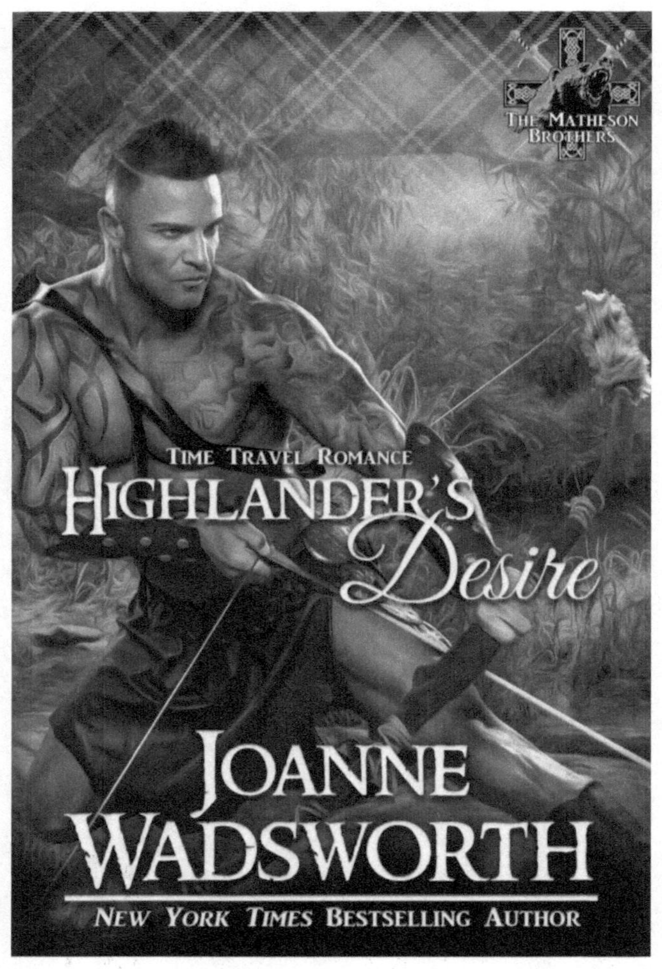

More Delicious Time Travel…

Highlander's Castle, Book 1

Scottish Historical Time Travel Romance

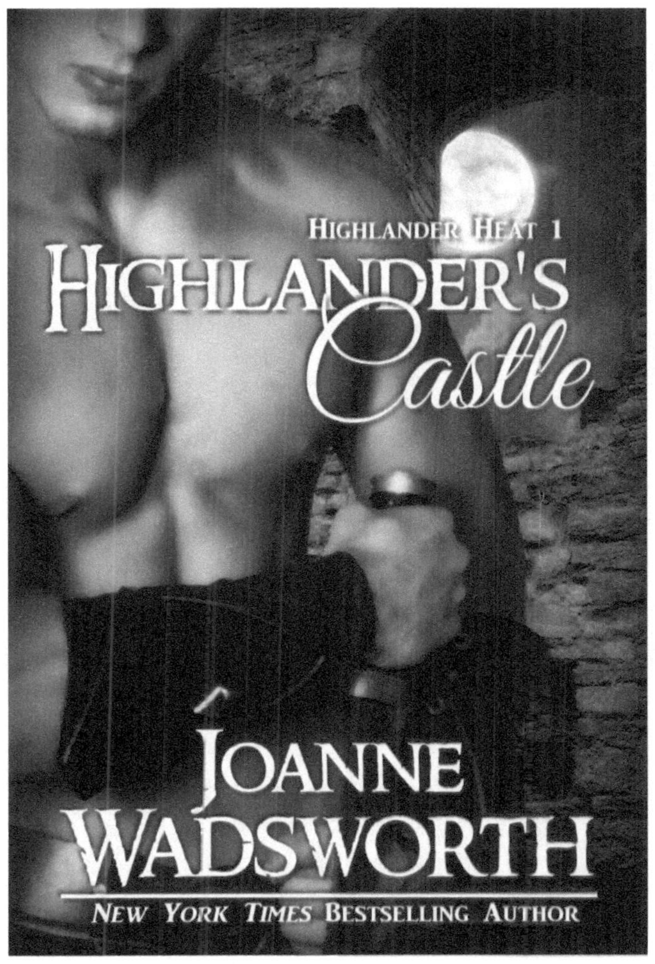

Young Adult Fantasy Romance

Protector, Book 1

Princesses of Myth Series

Want Some Alpha Bodyguards?

Billionaire Bodyguard Attraction, Book 1

Romantic Suspense

JOANNE WADSWORTH

Joanne Wadsworth is a *New York Times* and *USA Today* Bestselling Author who adores getting lost in the world of romance, no matter what era in time that might be. Hot alpha Highlanders hound her, demanding their stories are told and she's devoted to ensuring they meet their match, whether that be with a feisty lass from the present or far in the past.

Living on a tiny island at the bottom of the world, she calls New Zealand home. Big-dreamer, hoarder of chocolate, and addicted to juicy watermelons since the age of five, she chases after her four energetic children and has her own hunky hubby on the side.

So come and join in all the fun, because this kiwi girl promises to give you her "Hot-Highlander" oath, to bring you a heart-pounding, sexy adventure from the moment you turn the first page. This is where romance meets fantasy and adventure…

To learn more about Joanne and her works, visit
http://www.joannewadsworth.com